Mugby Junction (annot

by Charles Dickens

MUGBY JUNCTION

CHAPTER I

BARBOX BROTHERS

I.

"Guard! What place is this?"

"Mugby Junction, sir."

"A windy place!"

"Yes, it mostly is, sir."

"And looks comfortless indeed!"

"Yes, it generally does, sir."

"Is it a rainy night still?"

"Pours, sir."

"Open the door. I'll get out."

"You'll have, sir," said the guard, glistening with drops of wet, and looking at the tearful face of his watch by the light of his lantern as the traveller descended, "three minutes here."

"More, I think.--For I am not going on."

"Thought you had a through ticket, sir?"

"So I have, but I shall sacrifice the rest of it. I want my luggage."

"Please to come to the van and point it out, sir. Be good enough to look very sharp, sir. Not a moment to spare."

The guard hurried to the luggage van, and the traveller hurried after him. The guard got into it, and the traveller looked into it.

"Those two large black portmanteaus in the corner where your light shines. Those are mine."

"Name upon 'em, sir?"

"Barbox Brothers."

"Stand clear, sir, if you please. One. Two. Right!"

Lamp waved. Signal lights ahead already changing. Shriek from engine. Train gone.

"Mugby Junction!" said the traveller, pulling up the woollen muffler round his throat with both hands. "At past three o'clock of a tempestuous morning! So!"

He spoke to himself. There was no one else to speak to. Perhaps, though there had been any one else to speak to, he would have preferred to speak to himself. Speaking to himself he spoke to a man within five years of fifty either way, who had turned grey too soon, like a neglected fire; a man of pondering habit, brooding carriage of the head, and suppressed internal voice; a man with many indications on him of having been much alone.

He stood unnoticed on the dreary platform, except by the rain and by the wind. Those two vigilant assailants made a rush at him. "Very well," said he, yielding. "It signifies nothing to me to what quarter I turn my face."

Thus, at Mugby Junction, at past three o'clock of a tempestuous morning, the traveller went where the weather drove him.

Not but what he could make a stand when he was so minded, for, coming to the end of the roofed shelter (it is of considerable extent at Mugby Junction), and looking out upon the dark night, with a yet darker spirit- wing of storm beating its wild way through it, he faced about, and held his own as ruggedly in the difficult direction as he had held it in the easier one. Thus, with a steady step, the traveller went up and down, up and down, up and down, seeking nothing and finding it.

A place replete with shadowy shapes, this Mugby Junction in the black hours of the four-and-twenty. Mysterious goods trains, covered with palls and gliding on like vast weird funerals, conveying themselves guiltily away from the presence of the few lighted lamps, as if their freight had come to a secret and unlawful end. Half-miles of coal pursuing in a Detective manner, following when they lead, stopping when they stop, backing when they back. Red-hot embers showering out upon the ground, down this dark avenue, and down the other, as if torturing fires were being raked clear; concurrently, shrieks and groans and grinds invading the ear, as if the tortured were at the height of their suffering. Iron-barred cages full of cattle jangling by midway, the drooping beasts with horns entangled, eyes frozen with terror, and mouths too: at least they have long icicles (or what seem so) hanging from their lips. Unknown languages in the air, conspiring in red, green, and white characters. An earthquake, accompanied with thunder and lightning, going up express to London. Now, all quiet, all rusty, wind and rain in possession, lamps extinguished, Mugby Junction dead and indistinct, with its robe drawn over its head, like Caesar.

Now, too, as the belated traveller plodded up and down, a shadowy train went by him in the gloom which was no other than the train of a life. From whatsoever intangible deep cutting or dark tunnel it emerged, here it came, unsummoned and unannounced, stealing upon him, and passing away into obscurity. Here mournfully went by a child who had never had a childhood or known a parent, inseparable from a youth with a bitter sense of his namelessness, coupled to a man the enforced business of whose best years had been distasteful and oppressive, linked to an ungrateful friend, dragging after him a woman once beloved. Attendant, with many a clank and wrench, were lumbering cares, dark meditations, huge dim disappointments, monotonous years, a long jarring line of the discords of a solitary and unhappy existence.

"--Yours, sir?"

The traveller recalled his eyes from the waste into which they had been staring, and fell back a step or so under the abruptness, and perhaps the chance appropriateness, of the question.

"Oh! My thoughts were not here for the moment. Yes. Yes. Those two portmanteaus are mine. Are you a Porter?"

"On Porter's wages, sir. But I am Lamps."

The traveller looked a little confused.

"Who did you say you are?"

"Lamps, sir," showing an oily cloth in his hand, as farther explanation.

"Surely, surely. Is there any hotel or tavern here?"

"Not exactly here, sir. There is a Refreshment Room here, but--" Lamps, with a mighty serious look, gave his head a warning roll that plainly added--"but it's a blessed circumstance for you that it's not open."

"You couldn't recommend it, I see, if it was available?"

"Ask your pardon, sir. If it was--?"

"Open?"

"It ain't my place, as a paid servant of the company, to give my opinion on any of the company's toepics,"--he pronounced it more like toothpicks,--"beyond lamp-ile and cottons," returned Lamps in a confidential tone; "but, speaking as a man, I wouldn't recommend my father (if he was to come to life again) to go and try how he'd be treated at the Refreshment Room. Not speaking as a man, no, I would not."

The traveller nodded conviction. "I suppose I can put up in the town? There is a town here?" For the traveller (though a stay-at-home compared with most travellers) had been, like many others, carried on the steam winds and the iron tides through that Junction before, without having ever, as one might say, gone ashore there.

"Oh yes, there's a town, sir! Anyways, there's town enough to put up in. But," following the glance of the other at his luggage, "this is a very dead time of the night with us, sir. The deadest time. I might a'most call it our deadest and buriedest time."

"No porters about?"

"Well, sir, you see," returned Lamps, confidential again, "they in general goes off with the gas. That's how it is. And they seem to have overlooked you, through your walking to the furder end of the platform. But, in about twelve minutes or so, she may be up."

"Who may be up?"

"The three forty-two, sir. She goes off in a sidin' till the Up X passes, and then she"--here an air of hopeful vagueness pervaded Lamps--"does all as lays in her power."

"I doubt if I comprehend the arrangement."

"I doubt if anybody do, sir. She's a Parliamentary, sir. And, you see, a Parliamentary, or a Skirmishun--"

"Do you mean an Excursion?"

"That's it, sir.--A Parliamentary or a Skirmishun, she mostly does go off into a sidin'. But, when she can get a chance, she's whistled out of it, and she's whistled up into doin' all as,"--Lamps again wore the air of a highly sanguine man who hoped for the best,--"all as lays in her power."

He then explained that the porters on duty, being required to be in attendance on the Parliamentary matron in question, would doubtless turn up with the gas. In the meantime, if the gentleman would not very much object to the smell of lamp-oil, and would accept the warmth of his little room--The gentleman, being by this time very cold, instantly closed with the proposal.

A greasy little cabin it was, suggestive, to the sense of smell, of a cabin in a Whaler. But there was a bright fire burning in its rusty grate, and on the floor there stood a wooden stand of newly trimmed and lighted lamps, ready for carriage service. They made a bright show, and their light, and the warmth, accounted for the popularity of the room, as borne witness to by many impressions of velveteen trousers on a form by the fire, and many rounded smears and smudges of stooping velveteen shoulders on the adjacent wall. Various untidy shelves accommodated a quantity of lamps and oil-cans, and also a fragrant collection of what looked like the pocket-handkerchiefs of the whole lamp family.

As Barbox Brothers (so to call the traveller on the warranty of his luggage) took his seat upon the form, and warmed his now ungloved hands at the fire, he glanced aside at a little deal desk, much blotched with ink, which his elbow touched. Upon it were some scraps of coarse paper, and a superannuated steel pen in very reduced and gritty circumstances.

From glancing at the scraps of paper, he turned involuntarily to his host, and said, with some roughness:

"Why, you are never a poet, man?"

Lamps had certainly not the conventional appearance of one, as he stood modestly rubbing his squab nose with a handkerchief so exceedingly oily, that he might have been in the act of mistaking himself for one of his charges. He was a spare man of about the Barbox Brothers time of life, with his features whimsically drawn upward as if they were attracted by the roots of his hair. He had a peculiarly shining transparent complexion, probably occasioned by constant oleaginous application; and his attractive hair, being cut short, and being grizzled, and standing straight up on end as if it in its turn were attracted by some invisible magnet above it, the top of his head was not very unlike a lamp-wick.

"But, to be sure, it's no business of mine," said Barbox Brothers. "That was an impertinent observation on my part. Be what you like."

"Some people, sir," remarked Lamps in a tone of apology, "are sometimes what they don't like."

"Nobody knows that better than I do," sighed the other. "I have been what I don't like, all my life."

"When I first took, sir," resumed Lamps, "to composing little Comic-Songs--like--"

Barbox Brothers eyed him with great disfavour.

"--To composing little Comic-Songs-like--and what was more hard--to singing 'em afterwards," said Lamps, "it went against the grain at that time, it did indeed."

Something that was not all oil here shining in Lamps's eye, Barbox Brothers withdrew his own a little disconcerted, looked at the fire, and put a foot on the top bar. "Why did you do it, then?" he asked after a short pause; abruptly enough, but in a softer tone. "If you didn't want to do it, why did you do it? Where did you sing them? Public-house?"

To which Mr. Lamps returned the curious reply: "Bedside."

At this moment, while the traveller looked at him for elucidation, Mugby Junction started suddenly, trembled violently, and opened its gas eyes. "She's got up!" Lamps announced, excited. "What lays in her power is sometimes more, and sometimes less; but it's laid in her power to get up to-night, by George!"

The legend "Barbox Brothers," in large white letters on two black surfaces, was very soon afterwards trundling on a truck through a silent street, and, when the owner of the legend had shivered on the pavement half an hour, what time the porter's knocks at the Inn Door knocked up the whole town first, and the Inn last, he groped his way into the close air of a shut-up house, and so groped between the sheets of a shut-up bed that seemed to have been expressly refrigerated for him when last made.

II.

"You remember me, Young Jackson?"

"What do I remember if not you? You are my first remembrance. It was you who told me that was my name. It was you who told me that on every twentieth of December my life had a penitential anniversary in it called a birthday. I suppose the last communication was truer than the first!"

"What am I like, Young Jackson?"

"You are like a blight all through the year to me. You hard-lined, thin- lipped, repressive, changeless woman with a wax mask on. You are like the Devil to me; most of all when you teach me religious things, for you make me abhor them."

"You remember me, Mr. Young Jackson?" In another voice from another quarter.

"Most gratefully, sir. You were the ray of hope and prospering ambition in my life. When I attended your course, I believed that I should come to be a great healer, and I felt almost happy--even though I was still the one boarder in the house with that horrible mask, and ate and drank in silence and constraint with the mask before me, every day. As I had done every, every, every day, through my school-time and from my earliest recollection."

"What am I like, Mr. Young Jackson?"

"You are like a Superior Being to me. You are like Nature beginning to reveal herself to me. I hear you again, as one of the hushed crowd of young men kindling under the power of your presence and knowledge, and you bring into my eyes the only exultant tears that ever stood in them."

"You remember Me, Mr. Young Jackson?" In a grating voice from quite another quarter.

"Too well. You made your ghostly appearance in my life one day, and announced that its course was to be suddenly and wholly changed. You showed me which was my wearisome seat in the Galley of Barbox Brothers. (When they were, if they ever were, is unknown to me; there was nothing of them but the name when I bent to the oar.) You told me what I was to do, and what to be paid; you told me afterwards, at intervals of years, when I was to sign for the Firm, when I became a partner, when I became the Firm. I know no more of it, or of myself."

"What am I like, Mr. Young Jackson?"

"You are like my father, I sometimes think. You are hard enough and cold enough so to have brought up an acknowledged son. I see your scanty figure, your close brown suit, and your tight brown wig; but you, too, wear a wax mask to your death. You never by a chance remove it--it never by a chance falls off--and I know no more of you."

Throughout this dialogue, the traveller spoke to himself at his window in the morning, as he had spoken to himself at the Junction overnight. And as he had then looked in the darkness, a man who had turned grey too soon, like a neglected fire: so he now looked in the sun-light, an ashier grey, like a fire which the brightness of the sun put out.

The firm of Barbox Brothers had been some offshoot or irregular branch of the Public Notary and bill-broking tree. It had gained for itself a griping reputation before the days of Young Jackson, and the reputation had stuck to it and to him. As he had imperceptibly come into possession of the dim den up in the corner of a court off Lombard Street, on whose grimy windows the inscription Barbox Brothers had for many long years daily interposed itself between him and the sky, so he had insensibly found himself a personage held in chronic distrust, whom it was essential to screw tight to every transaction in which he engaged, whose word was never to be taken without his attested bond, whom all dealers with openly set up guards and wards against. This character had come upon him through no act of his own. It was as if the original Barbox had stretched himself down upon the office floor, and had thither caused to be conveyed Young Jackson in his sleep, and had there effected a metempsychosis and exchange of persons with him. The discovery--aided in its turn by the deceit of the only woman he had ever loved, and the deceit of the only friend he had ever made: who eloped from him to be married together--the discovery, so followed up, completed what his earliest rearing had begun. He shrank, abashed, within the form of Barbox, and lifted up his head and heart no more.

But he did at last effect one great release in his condition. He broke the oar he had plied so long, and he scuttled and sank the galley. He prevented the gradual retirement of an old conventional business from him, by taking the initiative and retiring from it. With enough to live on (though, after all, with not too much), he obliterated the firm of Barbox Brothers from the pages of the Post-Office Directory and the face of the earth, leaving nothing of it but its name on two portmanteaus.

"For one must have some name in going about, for people to pick up," he explained to Mugby High Street, through the Inn window, "and that name at least was real once. Whereas, Young Jackson!--Not to mention its being a sadly satirical misnomer for Old Jackson."

He took up his hat and walked out, just in time to see, passing along on the opposite side of the way, a velveteen man, carrying his day's dinner in a small bundle that might have been larger without suspicion of gluttony, and pelting away towards the Junction at a great pace.

"There's Lamps!" said Barbox Brothers. "And by the bye--"

Ridiculous, surely, that a man so serious, so self-contained, and not yet three days emancipated from a routine of drudgery, should stand rubbing his chin in the street, in a brown study about Comic Songs.

"Bedside?" said Barbox Brothers testily. "Sings them at the bedside? Why at the bedside, unless he goes to bed drunk? Does, I shouldn't wonder. But it's no business of mine. Let me see. Mugby Junction, Mugby Junction. Where shall I go next? As it came into my head last night when I woke from an uneasy sleep in the carriage and found myself here, I can go anywhere from here. Where shall I go? I'll go and look at the Junction by daylight. There's no hurry, and I may like the look of one Line better than another."

But there were so many Lines. Gazing down upon them from a bridge at the Junction, it was as if the concentrating Companies formed a great Industrial Exhibition of the works of extraordinary ground spiders that spun iron. And then so many of the Lines went such wonderful ways, so crossing and curving among one another, that the eye lost them. And then some of them appeared to start with the fixed intention of going five hundred miles, and all of a sudden gave it up at an insignificant barrier, or turned off into a workshop. And then others, like intoxicated men, went a little way very straight, and surprisingly slued round and came back again. And then others were so chock-full of trucks of coal, others were so blocked with trucks of casks, others were so gorged with trucks of ballast, others were so set apart for wheeled objects like immense iron cotton-reels: while others were so bright and clear, and others were so delivered over to rust and ashes and idle wheelbarrows out of work, with their legs in the air (looking much like their masters on strike), that there was no beginning, middle, or end to the bewilderment.

Barbox Brothers stood puzzled on the bridge, passing his right hand across the lines on his forehead, which multiplied while he looked down, as if the railway Lines were getting themselves photographed on that sensitive plate. Then was heard a distant ringing of bells and blowing of whistles. Then, puppet-looking heads of men popped out of boxes in perspective, and popped in again. Then, prodigious wooden razors, set up on end, began shaving the atmosphere. Then, several locomotive engines in several directions began to scream and be agitated. Then, along one avenue a train came in. Then, along another two trains appeared that didn't come in, but stopped without. Then, bits of trains broke off. Then, a struggling horse became involved with them. Then, the locomotives shared the bits of trains, and ran away with the whole.

"I have not made my next move much clearer by this. No hurry. No need to make up my mind to-day, or to-morrow, nor yet the day after. I'll take a walk."

It fell out somehow (perhaps he meant it should) that the walk tended to the platform at which he had alighted, and to Lamps's room. But Lamps was not in his room. A pair of velveteen shoulders were adapting themselves to one of the impressions on the wall by Lamps's fireplace, but otherwise the room was void. In passing back to get out of the station again, he learnt the cause of this vacancy, by catching sight of Lamps on the opposite line of railway, skipping along the top of a train, from carriage to carriage, and catching lighted namesakes thrown up to him by a coadjutor.

"He is busy. He has not much time for composing or singing Comic Songs this morning, I take it."

The direction he pursued now was into the country, keeping very near to the side of one great Line of railway, and within easy view of others. "I have half a mind,"' he said, glancing around, "to settle the question from this point, by saying, 'I'll take this set of rails, or that, or t'other, and stick to it.' They separate themselves from the confusion, out here, and go their ways."

Ascending a gentle hill of some extent, he came to a few cottages. There, looking about him as a very reserved man might who had never looked about him in his life before, he saw some six or eight young children come merrily trooping and whooping from one of the cottages, and disperse. But not until they had all turned at the little garden-gate, and kissed their hands to a face at the upper window: a low window enough, although the upper, for the cottage had but a story of one room above the ground.

Now, that the children should do this was nothing; but that they should do this to a face lying on the sill of the open window, turned towards them in a horizontal position, and apparently only a face, was something noticeable. He looked up at the window again. Could only see a very fragile, though a very bright face, lying on one cheek on the window-sill. The delicate smiling face of a girl or woman. Framed in long bright brown hair, round which was tied a light blue band or fillet, passing under the chin.

He walked on, turned back, passed the window again, shyly glanced up again. No change. He struck off by a winding branch-road at the top of the hill--which he must otherwise have descended--kept the cottages in view, worked his way round at a distance so as to come out once more into the main road, and be obliged to pass the cottages again. The face still lay on the window-sill, but not so much inclined towards him. And now there were a pair of delicate hands too. They had the action of performing on some musical instrument, and yet it produced no sound that reached his ears.

"Mugby Junction must be the maddest place in England," said Barbox Brothers, pursuing his way down the hill. "The first thing I find here is a Railway Porter who composes comic songs to sing at his bedside. The second thing I find here is a face, and a pair of hands playing a musical instrument that _don't_ play!"

The day was a fine bright day in the early beginning of November, the air was clear and inspiriting, and the landscape was rich in beautiful colours. The prevailing colours in the court off Lombard Street, London city, had been few and sombre. Sometimes, when the weather elsewhere was very bright indeed, the dwellers in those tents enjoyed a pepper-and-salt- coloured day or two, but their atmosphere's usual wear was slate or snuff coloured.

He relished his walk so well that he repeated it next day. He was a little earlier at the cottage than on the day before, and he could hear the children upstairs singing to a regular measure, and clapping out the time with their hands.

"Still, there is no sound of any musical instrument," he said, listening at the corner, "and yet I saw the performing hands again as I came by. What are the children singing? Why, good Lord, they can never be singing the multiplication table?"

They were, though, and with infinite enjoyment. The mysterious face had a voice attached to it, which occasionally led or set the children right. Its musical cheerfulness was delightful. The measure at length stopped, and was succeeded by a murmuring of young voices, and then by a short song which he made out to be about the current month of the year, and about what work it yielded to the labourers in the fields and farmyards. Then there was a stir of little feet, and the children came trooping and whooping out, as on the previous day. And again, as on the previous day, they all turned at the garden-gate, and kissed their hands--evidently to the face on the window-sill, though Barbox Brothers from his retired post of disadvantage at the corner could not see it.

But, as the children dispersed, he cut off one small straggler--a brown- faced boy with flaxen hair--and said to him:

"Come here, little one. Tell me, whose house is that?"

The child, with one swarthy arm held up across his eyes, half in shyness, and half ready for defence, said from behind the inside of his elbow:

"Phoebe's."

"And who," said Barbox Brothers, quite as much embarrassed by his part in the dialogue as the child could possibly be by his, "is Phoebe?"

To which the child made answer: "Why, Phoebe, of course."

The small but sharp observer had eyed his questioner closely, and had taken his moral measure. He lowered his guard, and rather assumed a tone with him: as having discovered him to be an unaccustomed person in the art of polite conversation.

"Phoebe," said the child, "can't be anybobby else but Phoebe. Can she?"

"No, I suppose not."

"Well," returned the child, "then why did you ask me?"

Deeming it prudent to shift his ground, Barbox Brothers took up a new position.

"What do you do there? Up there in that room where the open window is. What do you do there?"

"Cool," said the child.

"Eh?"

"Co-o-ol," the child repeated in a louder voice, lengthening out the word with a fixed look and great emphasis, as much as to say: "What's the use of your having grown up, if you're such a donkey as not to understand me?"

"Ah! School, school," said Barbox Brothers. "Yes, yes, yes. And Phoebe teaches you?"

The child nodded.

"Good boy."

"Tound it out, have you?" said the child.

"Yes, I have found it out. What would you do with twopence, if I gave it you?"

"Pend it."

The knock-down promptitude of this reply leaving him not a leg to stand upon, Barbox Brothers produced the twopence with great lameness, and withdrew in a state of humiliation.

But, seeing the face on the window-sill as he passed the cottage, he acknowledged its presence there with a gesture, which was not a nod, not a bow, not a removal of his hat from his head, but was a diffident compromise between or struggle with all three. The eyes in the face seemed amused, or cheered, or both, and the lips modestly said: "Good-day to you, sir."

"I find I must stick for a time to Mugby Junction," said Barbox Brothers with much gravity, after once more stopping on his return road to look at the Lines where they went their several ways so quietly. "I can't make up my mind yet which iron road to take. In fact, I must get a little accustomed to the Junction before I can decide."

So, he announced at the Inn that he was "going to stay on for the present," and improved his acquaintance with the Junction that night, and again next morning, and again next night and morning: going down to the station, mingling with the people there, looking about him down all the avenues of railway, and beginning to take an interest in the incomings and outgoings of the trains. At first, he often put his head into Lamps's little room, but he never found Lamps there. A pair or two of velveteen shoulders he usually found there, stooping over the fire, sometimes in connection with a clasped knife and a piece of bread and meat; but the answer to his inquiry, "Where's Lamps?" was, either that he was "t'other side the line," or, that it was his off-time, or (in the latter case) his own personal introduction to another Lamps who was not his Lamps. However, he was not so desperately set upon seeing Lamps now, but he bore the disappointment. Nor did he so wholly devote himself to his severe application to the study of Mugby Junction as to neglect exercise. On the contrary, he took a walk every day, and always the same walk. But the weather turned cold and wet again, and the window was never open.

III.

At length, after a lapse of some days, there came another streak of fine bright hardy autumn weather. It was a Saturday. The window was open, and the children were gone. Not surprising, this, for he had patiently watched and waited at the corner until they were gone.

"Good-day," he said to the face; absolutely getting his hat clear off his head this time.

"Good-day to you, sir."

"I am glad you have a fine sky again to look at."

"Thank you, sir. It is kind if you."

"You are an invalid, I fear?"

"No, sir. I have very good health."

"But are you not always lying down?"

"Oh yes, I am always lying down, because I cannot sit up! But I am not an invalid."

The laughing eyes seemed highly to enjoy his great mistake.

"Would you mind taking the trouble to come in, sir? There is a beautiful view from this window. And you would see that I am not at all ill--being so good as to care."

It was said to help him, as he stood irresolute, but evidently desiring to enter, with his diffident hand on the latch of the garden-gate. It did help him, and he went in.

The room upstairs was a very clean white room with a low roof. Its only inmate lay on a couch that brought her face to a level with the window. The couch was white too; and her simple dress or wrapper being light blue, like the band around her hair, she had an ethereal look, and a fanciful appearance of lying among clouds. He felt that she instinctively perceived him to be by habit a downcast taciturn man; it was another help to him to have established that understanding so easily, and got it over.

There was an awkward constraint upon him, nevertheless, as he touched her hand, and took a chair at the side of her couch.

"I see now," he began, not at all fluently, "how you occupy your hand. Only seeing you from the path outside, I thought you were playing upon something."

She was engaged in very nimbly and dexterously making lace. A lace-pillow lay upon her breast; and the quick movements and changes of her hands upon it, as she worked, had given them the action he had misinterpreted.

"That is curious," she answered with a bright smile. "For I often fancy, myself, that I play tunes while I am at work."

"Have you any musical knowledge?"

She shook her head.

"I think I could pick out tunes, if I had any instrument, which could be made as handy to me as my lace-pillow. But I dare say I deceive myself. At all events, I shall never know."

"You have a musical voice. Excuse me; I have heard you sing."

"With the children?" she answered, slightly colouring. "Oh yes. I sing with the dear children, if it can be called singing."

Barbox Brothers glanced at the two small forms in the room, and hazarded the speculation that she was fond of children, and that she was learned in new systems of teaching them?

"Very fond of them," she said, shaking her head again; "but I know nothing of teaching, beyond the interest I have in it, and the pleasure it gives me when they learn. Perhaps your overhearing my little scholars sing some of their lessons has led you so far astray as to think me a grand teacher? Ah! I thought so! No, I have only read and been told about that system. It seemed so pretty and pleasant, and to treat them so like the merry Robins they are, that I took up with it in my little way. You don't need to be told what a very little way mine is, sir," she added with a glance at the small forms and round the room.

All this time her hands were busy at her lace-pillow. As they still continued so, and as there was a kind of substitute for conversation in the click and play of its pegs, Barbox Brothers took the opportunity of observing her. He guessed her to be thirty. The charm of her transparent face and large bright brown eyes was, not that they were passively resigned, but that they were actively and thoroughly cheerful. Even her busy hands, which of their own thinness alone might have besought compassion, plied their task with a gay courage that made mere compassion an unjustifiable assumption of superiority, and an impertinence.

He saw her eyes in the act of rising towards his, and he directed his towards the prospect, saying: "Beautiful, indeed!"

"Most beautiful, sir. I have sometimes had a fancy that I would like to sit up, for once, only to try how it looks to an erect head. But what a foolish fancy that would be to encourage! It cannot look more lovely to any one than it does to me."

Her eyes were turned to it, as she spoke, with most delighted admiration and enjoyment. There was not a trace in it of any sense of deprivation.

"And those threads of railway, with their puffs of smoke and steam changing places so fast, make it so lively for me," she went on. "I think of the number of people who can go where they wish, on their business, or their pleasure; I remember that the puffs make signs to me that they are actually going while I look; and that enlivens the prospect with abundance of company, if I want company. There is the great Junction, too. I don't see it under the foot of the hill, but I can very often hear it, and I always know it is there. It seems to join me, in a way, to I don't know how many places and things that I shall never see."

With an abashed kind of idea that it might have already joined himself to something he had never seen, he said constrainedly: "Just so."

"And so you see, sir," pursued Phoebe, "I am not the invalid you thought me, and I am very well off indeed."

"You have a happy disposition," said Barbox Brothers: perhaps with a slight excusatory touch for his own disposition.

"Ah! But you should know my father," she replied. "His is the happy disposition!--Don't mind, sir!" For his reserve took the alarm at a step upon the stairs, and he distrusted that he would be set down for a troublesome intruder. "This is my father coming."

The door opened, and the father paused there.

"Why, Lamps!" exclaimed Barbox Brothers, starting from his chair. "How do you do, Lamps?"

To which Lamps responded: "The gentleman for Nowhere! How do you DO, sir?"

And they shook hands, to the greatest admiration and surprise of Lamp's daughter.

"I have looked you up half-a-dozen times since that night," said Barbox Brothers, "but have never found you."

"So I've heerd on, sir, so I've heerd on," returned Lamps. "It's your being noticed so often down at the Junction, without taking any train, that has begun to get you the name among us of the gentleman for Nowhere. No offence in my having called you by it when took by surprise, I hope, sir?"

"None at all. It's as good a name for me as any other you could call me by. But may I ask you a question in the corner here?"

Lamps suffered himself to be led aside from his daughter's couch by one of the buttons of his velveteen jacket.

"Is this the bedside where you sing your songs?"

Lamps nodded.

The gentleman for Nowhere clapped him on the shoulder, and they faced about again.

"Upon my word, my dear," said Lamps then to his daughter, looking from her to her visitor, "it is such an amaze to me, to find you brought acquainted with this gentleman, that I must (if this gentleman will excuse me) take a rounder."

Mr. Lamps demonstrated in action what this meant, by pulling out his oily handkerchief rolled up in the form of a ball, and giving himself an elaborate smear, from behind the right ear, up the cheek, across the forehead, and down the other cheek to behind his left ear. After this operation he shone exceedingly.

"It's according to my custom when particular warmed up by any agitation, sir," he offered by way of apology. "And really, I am throwed into that state of amaze by finding you brought acquainted with Phoebe, that I--that I think I will, if you'll excuse me, take another rounder." Which he did, seeming to be greatly restored by it.

They were now both standing by the side of her couch, and she was working at her lace-pillow. "Your daughter tells me," said Barbox Brothers, still in a half-reluctant shamefaced way, "that she never sits up."

"No, sir, nor never has done. You see, her mother (who died when she was a year and two months old) was subject to very bad fits, and as she had never mentioned to me that she was subject to fits, they couldn't be guarded against. Consequently, she dropped the baby when took, and this happened."

"It was very wrong of her," said Barbox Brothers with a knitted brow, "to marry you, making a secret of her infirmity.'

"Well, sir!" pleaded Lamps in behalf of the long-deceased. "You see, Phoebe and me, we have talked that over too. And Lord bless us! Such a number on us has our infirmities, what with fits, and what with misfits, of one sort and another, that if we confessed to 'em all before we got married, most of us might never get married."

"Might not that be for the better?"

"Not in this case, sir," said Phoebe, giving her hand to her father.

"No, not in this case, sir," said her father, patting it between his own.

"You correct me," returned Barbox Brothers with a blush; "and I must look so like a Brute, that at all events it would be superfluous in me to confess to that infirmity. I wish you would tell me a little more about yourselves. I hardly knew how to ask it of you, for I am conscious that I have a bad stiff manner, a dull discouraging way with me, but I wish you would."

"With all our hearts, sir," returned Lamps gaily for both. "And first of all, that you may know my name--"

"Stay!" interposed the visitor with a slight flush. "What signifies your name? Lamps is name enough for me. I like it. It is bright and expressive. What do I want more?"

"Why, to be sure, sir," returned Lamps. "I have in general no other name down at the Junction; but I thought, on account of your being here as a first-class single, in a private character, that you might--"

The visitor waved the thought away with his hand, and Lamps acknowledged the mark of confidence by taking another rounder.

"You are hard-worked, I take for granted?" said Barbox Brothers, when the subject of the rounder came out of it much dirtier than be went into it.

Lamps was beginning, "Not particular so"--when his daughter took him up.

"Oh yes, sir, he is very hard-worked. Fourteen, fifteen, eighteen hours a day. Sometimes twenty-four hours at a time."

"And you," said Barbox Brothers, "what with your school, Phoebe, and what with your lace-making--"

"But my school is a pleasure to me," she interrupted, opening her brown eyes wider, as if surprised to find him so obtuse. "I began it when I was but a child, because it brought me and other children into company, don't you see? That was not work. I carry it on still, because it keeps children about me. That is not work. I do it as love, not as work. Then my lace-pillow;" her busy hands had stopped, as if her argument required all her cheerful earnestness, but now went on again at the name; "it goes with my thoughts when I think, and it goes with my tunes when I hum any, and _that's_ not work. Why, you yourself thought it was music, you know, sir. And so it is to me."

"Everything is!" cried Lamps radiantly. "Everything is music to her, sir."

"My father is, at any rate," said Phoebe, exultingly pointing her thin forefinger at him. "There is more music in my father than there is in a brass band."

"I say! My dear! It's very fillyillially done, you know; but you are flattering your father," he protested, sparkling.

"No, I am not, sir, I assure you. No, I am not. If you could hear my father sing, you would know I am not. But you never will hear him sing, because he never sings to any one but me. However tired he is, he always sings to me when he comes home. When I lay here long ago, quite a poor little broken doll, he used to sing to me. More than that, he used to make songs, bringing in whatever little jokes we had between us. More than that, he often does so to this day. Oh! I'll tell of you, father, as the gentleman has asked about you. He is a poet, sir."

"I shouldn't wish the gentleman, my dear," observed Lamps, for the moment turning grave, "to carry away that opinion of your father, because it might look as if I was given to asking the stars in a molloncolly manner what they was up to. Which I wouldn't at once waste the time, and take the liberty, my dear."

"My father," resumed Phoebe, amending her text, "is always on the bright side, and the good side. You told me, just now, I had a happy disposition. How can I help it?"

"Well; but, my dear," returned Lamps argumentatively, "how can I help it? Put it to yourself sir. Look at her. Always as you see her now. Always working--and after all, sir, for but a very few shillings a week--always contented, always lively, always interested in others, of all sorts. I said, this moment, she was always as you see her now. So she is, with a difference that comes to much the same. For, when it is my Sunday off and the morning bells have done ringing, I hear the prayers and thanks read in the touchingest way, and I have the hymns sung to me--so soft, sir, that you couldn't hear 'em out of this room--in notes that seem to me, I am sure, to come from Heaven and go back to it."

It might have been merely through the association of these words with their sacredly quiet time, or it might have been through the larger association of the words with the Redeemer's presence beside the bedridden; but here her dexterous fingers came to a stop on the lace-pillow, and clasped themselves around his neck as he bent down. There was great natural sensibility in both father and daughter, the visitor could easily see; but each made it, for the other's sake, retiring, not demonstrative; and perfect cheerfulness, intuitive or acquired, was either the first or second nature of both. In a very few moments Lamps was taking another rounder with his comical features beaming, while Phoebe's laughing eyes (just a glistening speck or so upon their lashes) were again directed by turns to him, and to her work, and to Barbox Brothers.

"When my father, sir," she said brightly, "tells you about my being interested in other people, even though they know nothing about me--which, by the bye, I told you myself--you ought to know how that comes about. That's my father's doing."

"No, it isn't!" he protested.

"Don't you believe him, sir; yes, it is. He tells me of everything he sees down at his work. You would be surprised what a quantity he gets together for me every day. He looks into the carriages, and tells me how the ladies are dressed--so that I know all the fashions! He looks into the carriages, and tells me what pairs of lovers he sees, and what new- married couples on their wedding trip--so that I know all about that! He collects chance newspapers and books--so that I have plenty to read! He tells me about the sick people who are travelling to try to get better--so that I know all about them! In short, as I began by saying, he tells me everything he sees and makes out down at his work, and you can't think what a quantity he does see and make out."

"As to collecting newspapers and books, my dear," said Lamps, "it's clear I can have no merit in that, because they're not my perquisites. You see, sir, it's this way: A Guard, he'll say to me, 'Hallo, here you are, Lamps. I've saved this paper for your daughter. How is she a-going on?' A Head-Porter, he'll say to me, 'Here! Catch hold, Lamps. Here's a couple of wollumes for your daughter. Is she pretty much where she were?' And that's what makes it double welcome, you see. If she had a thousand pound in a box, they wouldn't trouble themselves about her; but being what she is--that is, you understand," Lamps added, somewhat hurriedly, "not having a thousand pound in a box--they take thought for her. And as concerning the young pairs, married and unmarried, it's only natural I should bring home what little I can about them, seeing that there's not a Couple of either sort in the neighbourhood that don't come of their own accord to confide in Phoebe."

She raised her eyes triumphantly to Barbox Brothers as she said:

"Indeed, sir, that is true. If I could have got up and gone to church, I don't know how often I should have been a bridesmaid. But, if I could have done that, some girls in love might have been jealous of me, and, as it is, no girl is jealous of me. And my pillow would not have been half as ready to put the piece of cake under, as I always find it," she added, turning her face on it with a light sigh, and a smile at her father.

The arrival of a little girl, the biggest of the scholars, now led to an understanding on the part of Barbox Brothers, that she was the domestic of the cottage, and had come to take active measures in it, attended by a pail that might have extinguished her, and a broom three times her height. He therefore rose to take his leave, and took it; saying that, if Phoebe had no objection, he would come again.

He had muttered that he would come "in the course of his walks." The course of his walks must have been highly favourable to his return, for he returned after an interval of a single day.

"You thought you would never see me any more, I suppose?" he said to Phoebe as he touched her hand, and sat down by her couch.

"Why should I think so?" was her surprised rejoinder.

"I took it for granted you would mistrust me."

"For granted, sir? Have you been so much mistrusted?"

"I think I am justified in answering yes. But I may have mistrusted, too, on my part. No matter just now. We were speaking of the Junction last time. I have passed hours there since the day before yesterday."

"Are you now the gentleman for Somewhere?" she asked with a smile.

"Certainly for Somewhere; but I don't yet know Where. You would never guess what I am travelling from. Shall I tell you? I am travelling from my birthday."

Her hands stopped in her work, and she looked at him with incredulous astonishment.

"Yes," said Barbox Brothers, not quite easy in his chair, "from my birthday. I am, to myself, an unintelligible book with the earlier chapters all torn out, and thrown away. My childhood had no grace of childhood, my youth had no charm of youth, and what can be expected from such a lost beginning?" His eyes meeting hers as they were addressed intently to him, something seemed to stir within his breast, whispering: "Was this bed a place for the graces of childhood and the charms of youth to take to kindly? Oh, shame, shame!"

"It is a disease with me," said Barbox Brothers, checking himself, and making as though he had a difficulty in swallowing something, "to go wrong about that. I don't know how I came to speak of that. I hope it is because of an old misplaced confidence in one of your sex involving an old bitter treachery. I don't know. I am all wrong together."

Her hands quietly and slowly resumed their work. Glancing at her, he saw that her eyes were thoughtfully following them.

"I am travelling from my birthday," he resumed, "because it has always been a dreary day to me. My first free birthday coming round some five or six weeks hence, I am travelling to put its predecessors far behind me, and to try to crush the day--or, at all events, put it out of my sight--by heaping new objects on it."

As he paused, she looked at him; but only shook her head as being quite at a loss.

"This is unintelligible to your happy disposition," he pursued, abiding by his former phrase as if there were some lingering virtue of self-defence in it. "I knew it would be, and am glad it is. However, on this travel of mine (in which I mean to pass the rest of my days, having abandoned all thought of a fixed home), I stopped, as you have heard from your father, at the Junction here. The extent of its ramifications quite confused me as to whither I should go, from here. I have not yet settled, being still perplexed among so many roads. What do you think I mean to do? How many of the branching roads can you see from your window?"

Looking out, full of interest, she answered, "Seven."

"Seven," said Barbox Brothers, watching her with a grave smile. "Well! I propose to myself at once to reduce the gross number to those very seven, and gradually to fine them down to one--the most promising for me--and to take that."

"But how will you know, sir, which is the most promising?" she asked, with her brightened eyes roving over the view.

"Ah!" said Barbox Brothers with another grave smile, and considerably improving in his ease of speech. "To be sure. In this way. Where your father can pick up so much every day for a good purpose, I may once and again pick up a little for an indifferent purpose. The gentleman for Nowhere must become still better known at the Junction. He shall continue to explore it, until he attaches something that he has seen, heard, or found out, at the head of each of the seven roads, to the road itself. And so his choice of a road shall be determined by his choice among his discoveries."

Her hands still busy, she again glanced at the prospect, as if it comprehended something that had not been in it before, and laughed as if it yielded her new pleasure.

"But I must not forget," said Barbox Brothers, "(having got so far) to ask a favour. I want your help in this expedient of mine. I want to bring you what I pick up at the heads of the seven roads that you lie here looking out at, and to compare notes with you about it. May I? They say two heads are better than one. I should say myself that probably depends upon the heads concerned. But I am quite sure, though we are so newly acquainted, that your head and your father's have found out better things, Phoebe, than ever mine of itself discovered."

She gave him her sympathetic right hand, in perfect rapture with his proposal, and eagerly and gratefully thanked him.

"That's well!" said Barbox Brothers. "Again I must not forget (having got so far) to ask a favour. Will you shut your eyes?"

Laughing playfully at the strange nature of the request, she did so.

"Keep them shut," said Barbox Brothers, going softly to the door, and coming back. "You are on your honour, mind, not to open you eyes until I tell you that you may?"

"Yes! On my honour."

"Good. May I take your lace-pillow from you for a minute?"

Still laughing and wondering, she removed her hands from it, and he put it aside.

"Tell me. Did you see the puffs of smoke and steam made by the morning fast-train yesterday on road number seven from here?"

"Behind the elm-trees and the spire?"

"That's the road," said Barbox Brothers, directing his eyes towards it.

"Yes. I watched them melt away."

"Anything unusual in what they expressed?"

"No!" she answered merrily.

"Not complimentary to me, for I was in that train. I went--don't open your eyes--to fetch you this, from the great ingenious town. It is not half so large as your lace-pillow, and lies easily and lightly in its place. These little keys are like the keys of a miniature piano, and you supply the air required with your left hand. May you pick out delightful music from it, my dear! For the present--you can open your eyes now--good- bye!"

In his embarrassed way, he closed the door upon himself, and only saw, in doing so, that she ecstatically took the present to her bosom and caressed it. The glimpse gladdened his heart, and yet saddened it; for so might she, if her youth had flourished in its natural course, having taken to her breast that day the slumbering music of her own child's voice.

CHAPTER II

BARBOX BROTHERS AND CO.

With good-will and earnest purpose, the gentleman for Nowhere began, on the very next day, his researches at the heads of the seven roads. The results of his researches, as he and Phoebe afterwards set them down in fair writing, hold their due places in this veracious chronicle. But they occupied a much longer time in the getting together than they ever will in the perusal. And this is probably the case with most reading matter, except when it is of that highly beneficial kind (for Posterity) which is "thrown off in a few moments of leisure" by the superior poetic geniuses who scorn to take prose pains.

It must be admitted, however, that Barbox by no means hurried himself. His heart being in his work of good-nature, he revelled in it. There was the joy, too (it was a true joy to him), of sometimes sitting by, listening to Phoebe as she picked out more and more discourse from her musical instrument, and as her natural taste and ear refined daily upon her first discoveries. Besides being a pleasure, this was an occupation, and in the course of weeks it consumed hours. It resulted that his dreaded birthday was close upon him before he had troubled himself any more about it.

The matter was made more pressing by the unforeseen circumstance that the councils held (at which Mr. Lamps, beaming most brilliantly, on a few rare occasions assisted) respecting the road to be selected were, after all, in nowise assisted by his investigations. For, he had connected this interest with this road, or that interest with the other, but could deduce no reason from it for giving any road the preference. Consequently, when the last council was holden, that part of the business stood, in the end, exactly where it had stood in the beginning.

"But, sir," remarked Phoebe, "we have only six roads after all. Is the seventh road dumb?"

"The seventh road? Oh!" said Barbox Brothers, rubbing his chin. "That is the road I took, you know, when I went to get your little present. That is its story. Phoebe."

"Would you mind taking that road again, sir?" she asked with hesitation.

"Not in the least; it is a great high-road after all."

"I should like you to take it," returned Phoebe with a persuasive smile, "for the love of that little present which must ever be so dear to me. I should like you to take it, because that road can never be again like any other road to me. I should like you to take it, in remembrance of your having done me so much good: of your having made me so much happier! If you leave me by the road you travelled when you went to do me this great kindness," sounding a faint chord as she spoke, "I shall feel, lying here watching at my window, as if it must conduct you to a prosperous end, and bring you back some day."

"It shall be done, my dear; it shall be done."

So at last the gentleman for Nowhere took a ticket for Somewhere, and his destination was the great ingenious town.

He had loitered so long about the Junction that it was the eighteenth of December when he left it. "High time," he reflected, as he seated himself in the train, "that I started in earnest! Only one clear day remains between me and the day I am running away from. I'll push onward for the hill-country to-morrow. I'll go to Wales."

It was with some pains that he placed before himself the undeniable advantages to be gained in the way of novel occupation for his senses from misty mountains, swollen streams, rain, cold, a wild seashore, and rugged roads. And yet he scarcely made them out as distinctly as he could have wished. Whether the poor girl, in spite of her new resource, her music, would have any feeling of loneliness upon her now--just at first--that she had not had before; whether she saw those very puffs of steam and smoke that he saw, as he sat in the train thinking of her; whether her face would have any pensive shadow on it as they died out of the distant view from her window; whether, in telling him he had done her so much good, she had not unconsciously corrected his old moody bemoaning of his station in life, by setting him thinking that a man might be a great healer, if he would, and yet not be a great doctor; these and other similar meditations got between him and his Welsh picture. There was within him, too, that dull sense of vacuity which follows separation from an object of interest, and cessation of a pleasant pursuit; and this sense, being quite new to him, made him restless. Further, in losing Mugby Junction, he had found himself again; and he was not the more enamoured of himself for having lately passed his time in better company.

But surely here, not far ahead, must be the great ingenious town. This crashing and clashing that the train was undergoing, and this coupling on to it of a multitude of new echoes, could mean nothing less than approach to the great station. It did mean nothing less. After some stormy flashes of town lightning, in the way of swift revelations of red brick blocks of houses, high red brick chimney-shafts, vistas of red brick railway arches, tongues of fire, blocks of smoke, valleys of canal, and hills if coal, there came the thundering in at the journey's end.

Having seen his portmanteaus safely housed in the hotel he chose, and having appointed his dinner hour, Barbox Brothers went out for a walk in the busy streets. And now it began to be suspected by him that Mugby Junction was a Junction of many branches, invisible as well as visible, and had joined him to an endless number of by-ways. For, whereas he would, but a little while ago, have walked these streets blindly brooding, he now had eyes and thoughts for a new external world. How the many toiling people lived, and loved, and died; how wonderful it was to consider the various trainings of eye and hand, the nice distinctions of sight and touch, that separated them into classes of workers, and even into classes of workers at subdivisions of one complete whole which combined their many intelligences and forces, though of itself but some cheap object of use or ornament in common life; how good it was to know that such assembling in a multitude on their part, and such contribution of their several dexterities towards a civilising end, did not deteriorate them as it was the fashion of the supercilious Mayflies of humanity to pretend, but engendered among them a self-respect, and yet a modest desire to be much wiser than they were (the first evinced in their well-balanced bearing and manner of speech when he stopped to ask a question; the second, in the announcements of their popular studies and amusements on the public walls); these considerations, and a host of such, made his walk a memorable one. "I too am but a little part of a great whole," he began to think; "and to be serviceable to myself and others, or to be happy, I must cast my interest into, and draw it out of, the common stock."

Although he had arrived at his journey's end for the day by noon, he had since insensibly walked about the town so far and so long that the lamplighters were now at their work in the streets, and the shops were sparkling up brilliantly. Thus reminded to turn towards his quarters, he was in the act of doing so, when a very little hand crept into his, and a very little voice said:

"Oh! if you please, I am lost!"

He looked down, and saw a very little fair-haired girl.

"Yes," she said, confirming her words with a serious nod. "I am indeed. I am lost!"

Greatly perplexed, he stopped, looked about him for help, descried none, and said, bending low.

"Where do you live, my child?"

"I don't know where I live," she returned. "I am lost."

"What is your name?"

"Polly."

"What is your other name?"

The reply was prompt, but unintelligible.

Imitating the sound as he caught it, he hazarded the guess, "Trivits."

"Oh no!" said the child, shaking her head. "Nothing like that."

"Say it again, little one."

An unpromising business. For this time it had quite a different sound.

He made the venture, "Paddens?"

"Oh no!" said the child. "Nothing like that."

"Once more. Let us try it again, dear."

A most hopeless business. This time it swelled into four syllables. "It can't be Tappitarver?" said Barbox Brothers, rubbing his head with his hat in discomfiture.

"No! It ain't," the child quietly assented.

On her trying this unfortunate name once more, with extraordinary efforts at distinctness, it swelled into eight syllables at least.

"Ah! I think," said Barbox Brothers with a desperate air of resignation, "that we had better give it up."

"But I am lost," said the child, nestling her little hand more closely in his, "and you'll take care of me, won't you?"

If ever a man were disconcerted by division between compassion on the one hand, and the very imbecility of irresolution on the other, here the man was. "Lost!" he repeated, looking down at the child. "I am sure I am. What is to be done?"

"Where do you live?" asked the child, looking up at him wistfully.

"Over there," he answered, pointing vaguely in the direction of his hotel.

"Hadn't we better go there?" said the child.

"Really," he replied, "I don't know but what we had."

So they set off, hand-in-hand. He, through comparison of himself against his little companion, with a clumsy feeling on him as if he had just developed into a foolish giant. She, clearly elevated in her own tiny opinion by having got him so neatly out of his embarrassment.

"We are going to have dinner when we get there, I suppose?" said Polly.

"Well," he rejoined, "I--Yes, I suppose we are."

"Do you like your dinner?" asked the child.

"Why, on the whole," said Barbox Brothers, "yes, I think I do."

"I do mine," said Polly. "Have you any brothers and sisters?"

"No. Have you?"

"Mine are dead."

"Oh!" said Barbox Brothers. With that absurd sense of unwieldiness of mind and body weighing him down, he would have not known how to pursue the conversation beyond this curt rejoinder, but that the child was always ready for him.

"What," she asked, turning her soft hand coaxingly in his, "are you going to do to amuse me after dinner?"

"Upon my soul, Polly," exclaimed Barbox Brothers, very much at a loss, "I have not the slightest idea!"

"Then I tell you what," said Polly. "Have you got any cards at your house?"

"Plenty," said Barbox Brothers in a boastful vein.

"Very well. Then I'll build houses, and you shall look at me. You mustn't blow, you know."

"Oh no," said Barbox Brothers. "No, no, no. No blowing. Blowing's not fair."

He flattered himself that he had said this pretty well for an idiotic monster; but the child, instantly perceiving the awkwardness of his attempt to adapt himself to her level, utterly destroyed his hopeful opinion of himself by saying compassionately: "What a funny man you are!"

Feeling, after this melancholy failure, as if he every minute grew bigger and heavier in person, and weaker in mind, Barbox gave himself up for a bad job. No giant ever submitted more meekly to be led in triumph by all- conquering Jack than he to be bound in slavery to Polly.

"Do you know any stories?" she asked him.

He was reduced to the humiliating confession: "No."

"What a dunce you must be, mustn't you?" said Polly.

He was reduced to the humiliating confession: "Yes."

"Would you like me to teach you a story? But you must remember it, you know, and be able to tell it right to somebody else afterwards."

He professed that it would afford him the highest mental gratification to be taught a story, and that he would humbly endeavour to retain it in his mind. Whereupon Polly, giving her hand a new little turn in his, expressive of settling down for enjoyment, commenced a long romance, of which every relishing clause began with the words: "So this," or, "And so this." As, "So this boy;" or, "So this fairy;" or, "And so this pie was four yards round, and two yards and a quarter deep." The interest of the romance was derived from the intervention of this fairy to punish this boy for having a greedy appetite. To achieve which purpose, this fairy made this pie, and this boy ate and ate and ate, and his cheeks swelled and swelled and swelled. There were many tributary circumstances, but the forcible interest culminated in the total consumption of this pie, and the bursting of this boy. Truly he was a fine sight, Barbox Brothers, with serious attentive face, and ear bent down, much jostled on the pavements of the busy town, but afraid of losing a single incident of the epic, lest he should be examined in it by-and-by, and found deficient.

Thus they arrived at the hotel. And there he had to say at the bar, and said awkwardly enough; "I have found a little girl!"

The whole establishment turned out to look at the little girl. Nobody knew her; nobody could make out her name, as she set it forth--except one chamber-maid, who said it was Constantinople--which it wasn't.

"I will dine with my young friend in a private room," said Barbox Brothers to the hotel authorities, "and perhaps you will be so good as to let the police know that the pretty baby is here. I suppose she is sure to be inquired for soon, if she has not been already. Come along, Polly."

Perfectly at ease and peace, Polly came along, but, finding the stairs rather stiff work, was carried up by Barbox Brothers. The dinner was a most transcendant success, and the Barbox sheepishness, under Polly's directions how to mince her meat for her, and how to diffuse gravy over the plate with a liberal and equal hand, was another fine sight.

"And now," said Polly, "while we are at dinner, you be good, and tell me that story I taught you."

With the tremors of a Civil Service examination upon him, and very uncertain indeed, not only as to the epoch at which the pie appeared in history, but also as to the measurements of that indispensable fact, Barbox Brothers made a shaky beginning, but under encouragement did very fairly. There was a want of breadth observable in his rendering of the cheeks, as well as the appetite, of the boy; and there was a certain tameness in his fairy, referable to an under-current of desire to account for her. Still, as the first lumbering performance of a good-humoured monster, it passed muster.

"I told you to be good," said Polly, "and you are good, ain't you?"

"I hope so," replied Barbox Brothers.

Such was his deference that Polly, elevated on a platform of sofa cushions in a chair at his right hand, encouraged him with a pat or two on the face from the greasy bowl of her spoon, and even with a gracious kiss. In getting on her feet upon her chair, however, to give him this last reward, she toppled forward among the dishes, and caused him to exclaim, as he effected her rescue: "Gracious Angels! Whew! I thought we were in the fire, Polly!"

"What a coward you are, ain't you?" said Polly when replaced.

"Yes, I am rather nervous," he replied. "Whew! Don't, Polly! Don't flourish your spoon, or you'll go over sideways. Don't tilt up your legs when you laugh, Polly, or you'll go over backwards. Whew! Polly, Polly, Polly," said Barbox Brothers, nearly succumbing to despair, "we are environed with dangers!"

Indeed, he could descry no security from the pitfalls that were yawning for Polly, but in proposing to her, after dinner, to sit upon a low stool. "I will, if you will," said Polly. So, as peace of mind should go before all, he begged the waiter to wheel aside the table, bring a pack of cards, a couple of footstools, and a screen, and close in Polly and himself before the fire, as it were in a snug room within the room. Then, finest sight of all, was Barbox Brothers on his footstool, with a pint decanter on the rug, contemplating Polly as she built successfully, and growing blue in the face with holding his breath, lest he should blow the house down.

"How you stare, don't you?" said Polly in a houseless pause.

Detected in the ignoble fact, he felt obliged to admit, apologetically:

"I am afraid I was looking rather hard at you, Polly."

"Why do you stare?" asked Polly.

"I cannot," he murmured to himself, "recall why.--I don't know, Polly."

"You must be a simpleton to do things and not know why, mustn't you?" said Polly.

In spite of which reproof, he looked at the child again intently, as she bent her head over her card structure, her rich curls shading her face. "It is impossible," he thought, "that I can ever have seen this pretty baby before. Can I have dreamed of her? In some sorrowful dream?"

He could make nothing of it. So he went into the building trade as a journeyman under Polly, and they built three stories high, four stories high; even five.

"I say! Who do you think is coming?" asked Polly, rubbing her eyes after tea.

He guessed: "The waiter?"

"No," said Polly, "the dustman. I am getting sleepy."

A new embarrassment for Barbox Brothers!

"I don't think I am going to be fetched to-night," said Polly. "What do you think?"

He thought not, either. After another quarter of an hour, the dustman not merely impending, but actually arriving, recourse was had to the Constantinopolitan chamber-maid: who cheerily undertook that the child should sleep in a comfortable and wholesome room, which she herself would share.

"And I know you will be careful, won't you," said Barbox Brothers, as a new fear dawned upon him, "that she don't fall out of bed?"

Polly found this so highly entertaining that she was under the necessity of clutching him round the neck with both arms as he sat on his footstool picking up the cards, and rocking him to and fro, with her dimpled chin on his shoulder.

"Oh, what a coward you are, ain't you?" said Polly. "Do you fall out of bed?"

"N--not generally, Polly."

"No more do I."

With that, Polly gave him a reassuring hug or two to keep him going, and then giving that confiding mite of a hand of hers to be swallowed up in the hand of the Constantinopolitan chamber-maid, trotted off, chattering, without a vestige of anxiety.

He looked after her, had the screen removed and the table and chairs replaced, and still looked after her. He paced the room for half an hour. "A most engaging little creature, but it's not that. A most winning little voice, but it's not that. That has much to do with it, but there is something more. How can it be that I seem to know this child? What was it she imperfectly recalled to me when I felt her touch in the street, and, looking down at her, saw her looking up at me?"

"Mr. Jackson!"

With a start he turned towards the sound of the subdued voice, and saw his answer standing at the door.

"Oh, Mr. Jackson, do not be severe with me! Speak a word of encouragement to me, I beseech you."

"You are Polly's mother."

"Yes."

Yes. Polly herself might come to this, one day. As you see what the rose was in its faded leaves; as you see what the summer growth of the woods was in their wintry branches; so Polly might be traced, one day, in a careworn woman like this, with her hair turned grey. Before him were the ashes of a dead fire that had once burned bright. This was the woman he had loved. This was the woman he had lost. Such had been the constancy of his imagination to her, so had Time spared her under its withholding, that now, seeing how roughly the inexorable hand had struck her, his soul was filled with pity and amazement.

He led her to a chair, and stood leaning on a corner of the chimney-piece, with his head resting on his hand, and his face half averted.

"Did you see me in the street, and show me to your child?" he asked.

"Yes."

"Is the little creature, then, a party to deceit?"

"I hope there is no deceit. I said to her, 'We have lost our way, and I must try to find mine by myself. Go to that gentleman, and tell him you are lost. You shall be fetched by-and-by.' Perhaps you have not thought how very young she is?"

"She is very self-reliant."

"Perhaps because she is so young."

He asked, after a short pause, "Why did you do this?"

"Oh, Mr. Jackson, do you ask me? In the hope that you might see something in my innocent child to soften your heart towards me. Not only towards me, but towards my husband."

He suddenly turned about, and walked to the opposite end of the room. He came back again with a slower step, and resumed his former attitude, saying:

"I thought you had emigrated to America?"

"We did. But life went ill with us there, and we came back."

"Do you live in this town?"

"Yes. I am a daily teacher of music here. My husband is a book-keeper."

"Are you--forgive my asking--poor?"

"We earn enough for our wants. That is not our distress. My husband is very, very ill of a lingering disorder. He will never recover--"

"You check yourself. If it is for want of the encouraging word you spoke of, take it from me. I cannot forget the old time, Beatrice."

"God bless you!" she replied with a burst of tears, and gave him her trembling hand.

"Compose yourself. I cannot be composed if you are not, for to see you weep distresses me beyond expression. Speak freely to me. Trust me."

She shaded her face with her veil, and after a little while spoke calmly. Her voice had the ring of Polly's.

"It is not that my husband's mind is at all impaired by his bodily suffering, for I assure you that is not the case. But in his weakness, and in his knowledge that he is incurably ill, he cannot overcome the ascendancy of one idea. It preys upon him, embitters every moment of his painful life, and will shorten it."

She stopping, he said again: "Speak freely to me. Trust me."

"We have had five children before this darling, and they all lie in their little graves. He believes that they have withered away under a curse, and that it will blight this child like the rest."

"Under what curse?"

"Both I and he have it on our conscience that we tried you very heavily, and I do not know but that, if I were as ill as he, I might suffer in my mind as he does. This is the constant burden:--'I believe, Beatrice, I was the only friend that Mr. Jackson ever cared to make, though I was so much his junior. The more influence he acquired in the business, the higher he advanced me, and I was alone in his private confidence. I came between him and you, and I took you from him. We were both secret, and the blow fell when he was wholly unprepared. The anguish it caused a man so compressed must have been terrible; the wrath it awakened inappeasable. So, a curse came to be invoked on our poor, pretty little flowers, and they fall.'"

"And you, Beatrice," he asked, when she had ceased to speak, and there had been a silence afterwards, "how say you?"

"Until within these few weeks I was afraid of you, and I believed that you would never, never forgive."

"Until within these few weeks," he repeated. "Have you changed your opinion of me within these few weeks?"

"Yes."

"For what reason?"

"I was getting some pieces of music in a shop in this town, when, to my terror, you came in. As I veiled my face and stood in the dark end of the shop, I heard you explain that you wanted a musical instrument for a bedridden girl. Your voice and manner were so softened, you showed such interest in its selection, you took it away yourself with so much tenderness of care and pleasure, that I knew you were a man with a most gentle heart. Oh, Mr. Jackson, Mr. Jackson, if you could have felt the refreshing rain of tears that followed for me!"

Was Phoebe playing at that moment on her distant couch? He seemed to hear her.

"I inquired in the shop where you lived, but could get no information. As I had heard you say that you were going back by the next train (but you did not say where), I resolved to visit the station at about that time of day, as often as I could, between my lessons, on the chance of seeing you again. I have been there very often, but saw you no more until to-day. You were meditating as you walked the street, but the calm expression of your face emboldened me to send my child to you. And when I saw you bend your head to speak tenderly to her, I prayed to GOD to forgive me for having ever brought a sorrow on it. I now pray to you to forgive me, and to forgive my husband. I was very young, he was young too, and, in the ignorant hardihood of such a time of life, we don't know what we do to those who have undergone more discipline. You generous man! You good man! So to raise me up and make nothing of my crime against you!"--for he would not see her on her knees, and soothed her as a kind father might have soothed an erring daughter--"thank you, bless you, thank you!"

When he next spoke, it was after having drawn aside the window curtain and looked out awhile. Then he only said:

"Is Polly asleep?"

"Yes. As I came in, I met her going away upstairs, and put her to bed myself."

"Leave her with me for to-morrow, Beatrice, and write me your address on this leaf of my pocket-book. In the evening I will bring her home to you--and to her father."

* * *

"Hallo!" cried Polly, putting her saucy sunny face in at the door next morning when breakfast was ready: "I thought I was fetched last night?"

"So you were, Polly, but I asked leave to keep you here for the day, and to take you home in the evening."

"Upon my word!" said Polly. "You are very cool, ain't you?"

However, Polly seemed to think it a good idea, and added: "I suppose I must give you a kiss, though you are cool."

The kiss given and taken, they sat down to breakfast in a highly conversational tone.

"Of course, you are going to amuse me?" said Polly.

"Oh, of course!" said Barbox Brothers.

In the pleasurable height of her anticipations, Polly found it indispensable to put down her piece of toast, cross one of her little fat knees over the other, and bring her little fat right hand down into her left hand with a business-like slap. After this gathering of herself together, Polly, by that time a mere heap of dimples, asked in a wheedling manner:

"What are we going to do, you dear old thing?"

"Why, I was thinking," said Barbox Brothers, "--but are you fond of horses, Polly?"

"Ponies, I am," said Polly, "especially when their tails are long. But horses--n-no--too big, you know."

"Well," pursued Barbox Brothers, in a spirit of grave mysterious confidence adapted to the importance of the consultation, "I did see yesterday, Polly, on the walls, pictures of two long-tailed ponies, speckled all over--"

"No, no, NO!" cried Polly, in an ecstatic desire to linger on the charming details. "Not speckled all over!"

"Speckled all over. Which ponies jump through hoops--"

"No, no, NO!" cried Polly as before. "They never jump through hoops!"

"Yes, they do. Oh, I assure you they do! And eat pie in pinafores--"

"Ponies eating pie in pinafores!" said Polly. "What a story-teller you are, ain't you?"

"Upon my honour.--And fire off guns."

(Polly hardly seemed to see the force of the ponies resorting to fire- arms.)

"And I was thinking," pursued the exemplary Barbox, "that if you and I were to go to the Circus where these ponies are, it would do our constitutions good."

"Does that mean amuse us?" inquired Polly. "What long words you do use, don't you?"

Apologetic for having wandered out of his depth, he replied:

"That means amuse us. That is exactly what it means. There are many other wonders besides the ponies, and we shall see them all. Ladies and gentlemen in spangled dresses, and elephants and lions and tigers."

Polly became observant of the teapot, with a curled-up nose indicating some uneasiness of mind.

"They never get out, of course," she remarked as a mere truism.

"The elephants and lions and tigers? Oh, dear no!"

"Oh, dear no!" said Polly. "And of course nobody's afraid of the ponies shooting anybody."

"Not the least in the world."

"No, no, not the least in the world," said Polly.

"I was also thinking," proceeded Barbox, "that if we were to look in at the toy-shop, to choose a doll--"

"Not dressed!" cried Polly with a clap of her hands. "No, no, NO, not dressed!"

"Full-dressed. Together with a house, and all things necessary for housekeeping--"

Polly gave a little scream, and seemed in danger of falling into a swoon of bliss.

"What a darling you are!" she languidly exclaimed, leaning back in her chair. "Come and be hugged, or I must come and hug you."

This resplendent programme was carried into execution with the utmost rigour of the law. It being essential to make the purchase of the doll its first feature--or that lady would have lost the ponies--the toy-shop expedition took precedence. Polly in the magic warehouse, with a doll as large as herself under each arm, and a neat assortment of some twenty more on view upon the counter, did indeed present a spectacle of indecision not quite compatible with unalloyed happiness, but the light cloud passed. The lovely specimen oftenest chosen, oftenest rejected, and finally abided by, was of Circassian descent, possessing as much boldness of beauty as was reconcilable with extreme feebleness of mouth, and combining a sky-blue silk pelisse with rose-coloured satin trousers, and a black velvet hat: which this fair stranger to our northern shores would seem to have founded on the portraits of the late Duchess of Kent. The name this distinguished foreigner brought with her from beneath the glowing skies of a sunny clime was (on Polly's authority) Miss Melluka, and the costly nature of her outfit as a housekeeper, from the Barbox coffers, may be inferred from the two facts that her silver tea-spoons were as large as her kitchen poker, and that the proportions of her watch exceeded those of her frying-pan. Miss Melluka was graciously pleased to express her entire approbation of the Circus, and so was Polly; for the ponies were speckled, and brought down nobody when they fired, and the savagery of the wild beasts appeared to be mere smoke--which article, in fact, they did produce in large quantities from their insides. The Barbox absorption in the general subject throughout the realisation of these delights was again a sight to see, nor was it less worthy to behold at dinner, when he drank to Miss Melluka, tied stiff in a chair opposite to Polly (the fair Circassian possessing an unbendable spine), and even induced the waiter to assist in carrying out with due decorum the prevailing glorious idea. To wind up, there came the agreeable fever of getting Miss Melluka and all her wardrobe and rich possessions into a fly with Polly, to be taken home. But, by that time, Polly had become unable to look upon such accumulated joys with waking eyes, and had withdrawn her consciousness into the wonderful Paradise of a child's sleep. "Sleep, Polly, sleep," said Barbox Brothers, as her head dropped on his shoulder; "you shall not fall out of this bed easily, at any rate!"

What rustling piece of paper he took from his pocket, and carefully folded into the bosom of Polly's frock, shall not be mentioned. He said nothing about it, and nothing shall be said about it. They drove to a modest suburb of the great ingenious town, and stopped at the fore-court of a small house. "Do not wake the child," said Barbox Brothers softly to the driver; "I will carry her in as she is."

Greeting the light at the opened door which was held by Polly's mother, Polly's bearer passed on with mother and child in to a ground-floor room. There, stretched on a sofa, lay a sick man, sorely wasted, who covered his eyes with his emaciated hand.

"Tresham," said Barbox in a kindly voice, "I have brought you back your Polly, fast asleep. Give me your hand, and tell me you are better."

The sick man reached forth his right hand, and bowed his head over the hand into which it was taken, and kissed it. "Thank you, thank you! I may say that I am well and happy."

"That's brave," said Barbox. "Tresham, I have a fancy--Can you make room for me beside you here?"

He sat down on the sofa as he said the words, cherishing the plump peachey cheek that lay uppermost on his shoulder.

"I have a fancy, Tresham (I am getting quite an old fellow now, you know, and old fellows may take fancies into their heads sometimes), to give up Polly, having found her, to no one but you. Will you take her from me?"

As the father held out his arms for the child, each of the two men looked steadily at the other.

"She is very dear to you, Tresham?"

"Unutterably dear."

"God bless her! It is not much, Polly," he continued, turning his eyes upon her peaceful face as he apostrophized her, "it is not much, Polly, for a blind and sinful man to invoke a blessing on something so far better than himself as a little child is; but it would be much--much upon his cruel head, and much upon his guilty soul--if he could be so wicked as to invoke a curse. He had better have a millstone round his neck, and be cast into the deepest sea. Live and thrive, my pretty baby!" Here he kissed her. "Live and prosper, and become in time the mother of other little children, like the Angels who behold The Father's face!"

He kissed her again, gave her up gently to both her parents, and went out.

But he went not to Wales. No, he never went to Wales. He went straightway for another stroll about the town, and he looked in upon the people at their work, and at their play, here, there, every-there, and where not. For he was Barbox Brothers and Co. now, and had taken thousands of partners into the solitary firm.

He had at length got back to his hotel room, and was standing before his fire refreshing himself with a glass of hot drink which he had stood upon the chimney-piece, when he heard the town clocks striking, and, referring to his watch, found the evening to have so slipped away, that they were striking twelve. As he put up his watch again, his eyes met those of his reflection in the chimney-glass.

"Why, it's your birthday already," he said, smiling. "You are looking very well. I wish you many happy returns of the day."

He had never before bestowed that wish upon himself. "By Jupiter!" he discovered, "it alters the whole case of running away from one's birthday! It's a thing to explain to Phoebe. Besides, here is quite a long story to tell her, that has sprung out of the road with no story. I'll go back, instead of going on. I'll go back by my friend Lamps's Up X presently."

He went back to Mugby Junction, and, in point of fact, he established himself at Mugby Junction. It was the convenient place to live in, for brightening Phoebe's life. It was the convenient place to live in, for having her taught music by Beatrice. It was the convenient place to live in, for occasionally borrowing Polly. It was the convenient place to live in, for being joined at will to all sorts of agreeable places and persons. So, he became settled there, and, his house standing in an elevated situation, it is noteworthy of him in conclusion, as Polly herself might (not irreverently) have put it:

"There was an Old Barbox who lived on a hill, And if he ain't gone, he lives there still."

Here follows the substance of what was seen, heard, or otherwise picked up, by the gentleman for Nowhere, in his careful study of the Junction.

CHAPTER III

THE BOY AT MUGBY

I am the boy at Mugby. That's about what I am.

You don't know what I mean? What a pity! But I think you do. I think you must. Look here. I am the boy at what is called The Refreshment Room at Mugby Junction, and what's proudest boast is, that it never yet refreshed a mortal being.

Up in a corner of the Down Refreshment Room at Mugby Junction, in the height of twenty-seven cross draughts (I've often counted 'em while they brush the First-Class hair twenty-seven ways), behind the bottles, among the glasses, bounded on the nor'west by the beer, stood pretty far to the right of a metallic object that's at times the tea-urn and at times the soup-tureen, according to the nature of the last twang imparted to its contents which are the same groundwork, fended off from the traveller by a barrier of stale sponge-cakes erected atop of the counter, and lastly exposed sideways to the glare of Our Missis's eye--you ask a Boy so sitiwated, next time you stop in a hurry at Mugby, for anything to drink; you take particular notice that he'll try to seem not to hear you, that he'll appear in a absent manner to survey the Line through a transparent medium composed of your head and body, and that he won't serve you as long as you can possibly bear it. That's me.

What a lark it is! We are the Model Establishment, we are, at Mugby. Other

Refreshment Rooms send their imperfect young ladies up to be finished off by our Missis. For some of the young ladies, when they're new to the business, come into it mild! Ah! Our Missis, she soon takes that out of 'em. Why, I originally come into the business meek myself. But Our Missis, she soon took that out of me.

What a delightful lark it is! I look upon us Refreshmenters as ockipying the only proudly independent footing on the Line. There's Papers, for instance,-- my honourable friend, if he will allow me to call him so,--him as belongs to Smith's bookstall. Why, he no more dares to be up to our Refreshmenting games than he dares to jump a top of a locomotive with her steam at full pressure, and cut away upon her alone, driving himself, at limited-mail speed. Papers, he'd get his head punched at every compartment, first, second, and third, the whole length of a train, if he was to ventur to imitate my demeanour. It's the same with the porters, the same with the guards, the same with the ticket clerks, the same the whole way up to the secretary, traffic-manager, or very chairman. There ain't a one among 'em on the nobly independent footing we are. Did you ever catch one of them, when you wanted anything of him, making a system of surveying the Line through a transparent medium composed of your head and body? I should hope not.

You should see our Bandolining Room at Mugby Junction. It's led to by the door behind the counter, which you'll notice usually stands ajar, and it's the room where Our Missis and our young ladies Bandolines their hair. You should see 'em at it, betwixt trains, Bandolining away, as if they was anointing themselves for the combat. When you're telegraphed, you should see their noses all a-going up with scorn, as if it was a part of the working of the same Cooke and Wheatstone electrical machinery. You should hear Our Missis give the word, "Here comes the Beast to be Fed!" and then you should see 'em indignantly skipping across the Line, from the Up to the Down, or Wicer Warsaw, and begin to pitch the stale pastry into the plates, and chuck the sawdust sangwiches under the glass covers, and get out the--ha, ha, ha!--the sherry,--O my eye, my eye!--for your Refreshment.

It's only in the Isle of the Brave and Land of the Free (by which, of course, I mean to say Britannia) that Refreshmenting is so effective, so 'olesome, so constitutional a check upon the public. There was a Foreigner, which having politely, with his hat off, beseeched our young ladies and Our Missis for "a leetel gloss host prarndee," and having had the Line surveyed through him by all and no other acknowledgment, was a- proceeding at last to help himself, as seems to be the custom in his own country, when Our Missis, with her hair almost a-coming un-Bandolined with rage, and her eyes omitting sparks, flew at him, cotched the decanter out of his hand, and said, "Put it down! I won't allow that!" The foreigner turned pale, stepped back with his arms stretched out in front of him, his hands clasped, and his shoulders riz, and exclaimed: "Ah! Is it possible, this! That these disdaineous females and this ferocious old woman are placed here by the administration, not only to empoison the voyagers, but to affront them! Great Heaven! How arrives it? The English people. Or is he then a slave? Or idiot?" Another time, a merry, wideawake American gent had tried the sawdust and spit it out, and had tried the Sherry and spit that out, and had tried in vain to sustain exhausted natur upon Butter-Scotch, and had been rather extra Bandolined and Line-surveyed through, when, as the bell was ringing and he paid Our Missis, he says, very loud and good-tempered: "I tell Yew what 'tis, ma'arm. I la'af. Theer! I la'af. I Dew. I oughter ha' seen most things, for I hail from the Onlimited side of the Atlantic Ocean, and I haive travelled right slick over the Limited, head on through Jeerusalemm and the East, and likeways France and Italy, Europe Old World, and am now upon the track to the Chief Europian Village; but such an Institution as Yew, and Yewer young ladies, and Yewer fixin's solid and liquid, afore the glorious Tarnal I never did see yet! And if I hain't found the eighth wonder of monarchical Creation, in finding Yew and Yewer young ladies, and Yewer fixin's solid and liquid, all as aforesaid, established in a country where the people air not absolute Loo- naticks, I am Extra Double Darned with a Nip and Frizzle to the innermostest grit! Wheerfur--Theer!--I la'af! I Dew, ma'arm. I la'af!" And so he went, stamping and shaking his sides, along the platform all the way to his own compartment.

I think it was her standing up agin the Foreigner as giv' Our Missis the idea of going over to France, and droring a comparison betwixt Refreshmenting as followed among the frog-eaters, and Refreshmenting as triumphant in the Isle of the Brave and Land of the Free (by which, of course, I mean to say agin, Britannia). Our young ladies, Miss Whiff, Miss Piff, and Mrs. Sniff, was unanimous opposed to her going; for, as they says to Our Missis one and all, it is well beknown to the hends of the herth as no other nation except Britain has a idea of anythink, but above all of business. Why then should you tire yourself to prove what is already proved? Our Missis, however (being a teazer at all pints) stood out grim obstinate, and got a return pass by Southeastern Tidal, to go right through, if such should be her dispositions, to Marseilles.

Sniff is husband to Mrs. Sniff, and is a regular insignificant cove. He looks arter the sawdust department in a back room, and is sometimes, when we are very hard put to it, let behind the counter with a corkscrew; but never when it can be helped, his demeanour towards the public being disgusting servile. How Mrs. Sniff ever come so far to lower herself as to marry him, I don't know; but I suppose he does, and I should think he wished he didn't, for he leads a awful life. Mrs. Sniff couldn't be much harder with him if he was public. Similarly, Miss Whiff and Miss Piff, taking the tone of Mrs. Sniff, they shoulder Sniff about when he is let in with a corkscrew, and they whisk things out of his hands when in his servility he is a-going to let the public have 'em, and they snap him up when in the crawling baseness of his spirit he is a-going to answer a public question, and they drore more tears into his eyes than ever the mustard does which he all day long lays on to the sawdust. (But it ain't strong.) Once, when Sniff had the repulsiveness to reach across to get the milk-pot to hand over for a baby, I see Our Missis in her rage catch him by both his shoulders, and spin him out into the Bandolining Room.

But Mrs. Sniff,--how different! She's the one! She's the one as you'll notice to be always looking another way from you, when you look at her. She's the one with the small waist buckled in tight in front, and with the lace cuffs at her wrists, which she puts on the edge of the counter before her, and stands a smoothing while the public foams. This smoothing the cuffs and looking another way while the public foams is the last accomplishment taught to the young ladies as come to Mugby to be finished by Our Missis; and it's always taught by Mrs. Sniff.

When Our Missis went away upon her journey, Mrs. Sniff was left in charge. She did hold the public in check most beautiful! In all my time, I never see half so many cups of tea given without milk to people as wanted it with, nor half so many cups of tea with milk given to people as wanted it without. When foaming ensued, Mrs. Sniff would say: "Then you'd better settle it among yourselves, and change with one another." It was a most highly delicious lark. I enjoyed the Refreshmenting business more than ever, and was so glad I had took to it when young.

Our Missis returned. It got circulated among the young ladies, and it as it might be penetrated to me through the crevices of the Bandolining Room, that she had Orrors to reveal, if revelations so contemptible could be dignified with the name. Agitation become awakened. Excitement was up in the stirrups. Expectation stood a-tiptoe. At length it was put forth that on our slacked evening in the week, and at our slackest time of that evening betwixt trains, Our Missis would give her views of foreign Refreshmenting, in the Bandolining Room.

It was arranged tasteful for the purpose. The Bandolining table and glass was hid in a corner, a arm-chair was elevated on a packing-case for Our Missis's ockypation, a table and a tumbler of water (no sherry in it, thankee) was placed beside it. Two of the pupils, the season being autumn, and hollyhocks and dahlias being in, ornamented the wall with three devices in those flowers. On one might be read, "MAY ALBION NEVER LEARN;" on another "KEEP THE PUBLIC DOWN;" on another, "OUR REFRESHMENTING CHARTER." The whole had a beautiful appearance, with which the beauty of the sentiments corresponded.

On Our Missis's brow was wrote Severity, as she ascended the fatal platform. (Not that that was anythink new.) Miss Whiff and Miss Piff sat at her feet. Three chairs from the Waiting Room might have been perceived by a average eye, in front of her, on which the pupils was accommodated. Behind them a very close observer might have discerned a Boy. Myself.

"Where," said Our Missis, glancing gloomily around, "is Sniff?"

"I thought it better," answered Mrs. Sniff, "that he should not be let to come in. He is such an Ass."

"No doubt," assented Our Missis. "But for that reason is it not desirable to improve his mind?"

"Oh, nothing will ever improve him," said Mrs. Sniff.

"However," pursued Our Missis, "call him in, Ezekiel."

I called him in. The appearance of the low-minded cove was hailed with disapprobation from all sides, on account of his having brought his corkscrew with him. He pleaded "the force of habit."

"The force!" said Mrs. Sniff. "Don't let us have you talking about force, for Gracious' sake. There! Do stand still where you are, with your back against the wall."

He is a smiling piece of vacancy, and he smiled in the mean way in which he will even smile at the public if he gets a chance (language can say no meaner of him), and he stood upright near the door with the back of his head agin the wall, as if he was a waiting for somebody to come and measure his heighth for the Army.

"I should not enter, ladies," says Our Missis, "on the revolting disclosures I am about to make, if it was not in the hope that they will cause you to be yet more implacable in the exercise of the power you wield in a constitutional country, and yet more devoted to the constitutional motto which I see before me,"--it was behind her, but the words sounded better so,--"'May Albion never learn!'"

Here the pupils as had made the motto admired it, and cried, "Hear! Hear! Hear!" Sniff, showing an inclination to join in chorus, got himself frowned down by every brow.

"The baseness of the French," pursued Our Missis, "as displayed in the fawning nature of their Refreshmenting, equals, if not surpasses, anythink as was ever heard of the baseness of the celebrated Bonaparte."

Miss Whiff, Miss Piff, and me, we drored a heavy breath, equal to saying, "We thought as much!" Miss Whiff and Miss Piff seeming to object to my droring mine along with theirs, I drored another to aggravate 'em.

"Shall I be believed," says Our Missis, with flashing eyes, "when I tell you that no sooner had I set my foot upon that treacherous shore--"

Here Sniff, either bursting out mad, or thinking aloud, says, in a low voice: "Feet. Plural, you know."

The cowering that come upon him when he was spurned by all eyes, added to his being beneath contempt, was sufficient punishment for a cove so grovelling. In the midst of a silence rendered more impressive by the turned-up female noses with which it was pervaded, Our Missis went on:

"Shall I be believed when I tell you, that no sooner had I landed," this word with a killing look at Sniff, "on that treacherous shore, than I was ushered into a Refreshment Room where there were--I do not exaggerate--actually eatable things to eat?"

A groan burst from the ladies. I not only did myself the honour of jining, but also of lengthening it out.

"Where there were," Our Missis added, "not only eatable things to eat, but also drinkable things to drink?"

A murmur, swelling almost into a scream, ariz. Miss Piff, trembling with indignation, called out, "Name?"

"I will name," said Our Missis. "There was roast fowls, hot and cold; there was smoking roast veal surrounded with browned potatoes; there was hot soup with (again I ask shall I be credited?) nothing bitter in it, and no flour to choke off the consumer; there was a variety of cold dishes set off with jelly; there was salad; there was--mark me! fresh pastry, and that of a light construction; there was a luscious show of fruit; there was bottles and decanters of sound small wine, of every size, and adapted to every pocket; the same odious statement will apply to brandy; and these were set out upon the counter so that all could help themselves."

Our Missis's lips so quivered, that Mrs. Sniff, though scarcely less convulsed than she were, got up and held the tumbler to them.

"This," proceeds Our Missis, "was my first unconstitutional experience. Well would it have been if it had been my last and worst. But no. As I proceeded farther into that enslaved and ignorant land, its aspect became more hideous. I need not explain to this assembly the ingredients and formation of the British Refreshment sangwich?"

Universal laughter,--except from Sniff, who, as sangwich-cutter, shook his head in a state of the utmost dejection as he stood with it agin the wall.

"Well!" said Our Missis, with dilated nostrils. "Take a fresh, crisp, long, crusty penny loaf made of the whitest and best flour. Cut it longwise through the middle. Insert a fair and nicely fitting slice of ham. Tie a smart piece of ribbon round the middle of the whole to bind it together. Add at one end a neat wrapper of clean white paper by which to hold it. And the universal French Refreshment sangwich busts on your disgusted vision."

A cry of "Shame!" from all--except Sniff, which rubbed his stomach with a soothing hand.

"I need not," said Our Missis, "explain to this assembly the usual formation and fitting of the British Refreshment Room?"

No, no, and laughter. Sniff agin shaking his head in low spirits agin the wall.

"Well," said Our Missis, "what would you say to a general decoration of everythink, to hangings (sometimes elegant), to easy velvet furniture, to abundance of little tables, to abundance of little seats, to brisk bright waiters, to great convenience, to a pervading cleanliness and tastefulness positively addressing the public, and making the Beast thinking itself worth the pains?"

Contemptuous fury on the part of all the ladies. Mrs. Sniff looking as if she wanted somebody to hold her, and everbody else looking as if they'd rayther not.

"Three times," said Our Missis, working herself into a truly terrimenjious state,--"three times did I see these shameful things, only between the coast and Paris, and not counting either: at Hazebroucke, at Arras, at Amiens. But worse remains. Tell me, what would you call a person who should propose in England that there should be kept, say at our own model Mugby Junction, pretty baskets, each holding an assorted cold lunch and dessert for one, each at a certain fixed price, and each within a passenger's power to take away, to empty in the carriage at perfect leisure, and to return at another station fifty or a hundred miles farther on?"

There was disagreement what such a person should be called. Whether revolutionise, atheist, Bright (I said him), or Un-English. Miss Piff screeched her shrill opinion last, in the words: "A malignant maniac!"

"I adopt," says Our Missis, "the brand set upon such a person by the righteous indignation of my friend Miss Piff. A malignant maniac. Know, then, that that malignant maniac has sprung from the congenial soil of France, and that his malignant madness was in unchecked action on this same part of my journey."

I noticed that Sniff was a-rubbing his hands, and that Mrs. Sniff had got her eye upon him. But I did not take more particular notice, owing to the excited state in which the young ladies was, and to feeling myself called upon to keep it up with a howl.

"On my experience south of Paris," said Our Missis, in a deep tone, "I will not expatiate. Too loathsome were the task! But fancy this. Fancy a guard coming round, with the train at full speed, to inquire how many for dinner. Fancy his telegraphing forward the number of dinners. Fancy every one expected, and the table elegantly laid for the complete party. Fancy a charming dinner, in a charming room, and the head-cook, concerned for the honour of every dish, superintending in his clean white jacket and cap. Fancy the Beast travelling six hundred miles on end, very fast, and with great punctuality, yet being taught to expect all this to be done for it!"

A spirited chorus of "The Beast!"

I noticed that Sniff was agin a-rubbing his stomach with a soothing hand, and that he had drored up one leg. But agin I didn't take particular notice, looking on myself as called upon to stimulate public feeling. It being a lark besides.

"Putting everything together," said Our Missis, "French Refreshmenting comes to this, and oh, it comes to a nice total! First: eatable things to eat, and drinkable things to drink."

A groan from the young ladies, kep' up by me.

"Second: convenience, and even elegance."

Another groan from the young ladies, kep' up by me.

"Third: moderate charges."

This time a groan from me, kep' up by the young ladies.

"Fourth:--and here," says Our Missis, "I claim your angriest sympathy,--attention, common civility, nay, even politeness!"

Me and the young ladies regularly raging mad all together.

"And I cannot in conclusion," says Our Missis, with her spitefullest sneer, "give you a completer pictur of that despicable nation (after what I have related), than assuring you that they wouldn't bear our constitutional ways and noble independence at Mugby Junction, for a single month, and that they would turn us to the right-about and put another system in our places, as soon as look at us; perhaps sooner, for I do not believe they have the good taste to care to look at us twice."

The swelling tumult was arrested in its rise. Sniff, bore away by his servile disposition, had drored up his leg with a higher and a higher relish, and was now discovered to be waving his corkscrew over his head. It was at this moment that Mrs. Sniff, who had kep' her eye upon him like the fabled obelisk, descended on her victim. Our Missis followed them both out, and cries was heard in the sawdust department.

You come into the Down Refreshment Room, at the Junction, making believe you don't know me, and I'll pint you out with my right thumb over my shoulder which is Our Missis, and which is Miss Whiff, and which is Miss Piff, and which is Mrs. Sniff. But you won't get a chance to see Sniff, because he disappeared that night. Whether he perished, tore to pieces, I cannot say; but his corkscrew alone remains, to bear witness to the servility of his disposition.

Sir Arthur Conan Doyle

Early life

Arthur Ignatius Conan Doyle was born on 22 May 1859 at 11 Picardy Place, Edinburgh, Scotland.[2][3] His father, Charles Altamont Doyle, was English, of Irish Catholic descent, and his mother, Mary (née Foley), was Irish Catholic. His parents married in 1855.[4] In 1864 the family dispersed due to Charles's growing alcoholism and the children were temporarily housed across Edinburgh. In 1867, the family came together again and lived in squalid tenement flats at 3 Sciennes Place.[5]

Supported by wealthy uncles, Doyle was sent to the Jesuit preparatory school Hodder Place, Stonyhurst, at the age of nine (1868–70). He then went on to Stonyhurst College until 1875. From 1875 to 1876, he was educated at the Jesuit school Stella Matutina in Feldkirch, Austria.[5] By the time he left, he had rejected religion and become an agnostic,[6] though he would eventually become a spiritualist mystic.[7]

Doyle's father died in 1893, in the Crichton Royal, Dumfries, after many years of psychiatric illness.[8][9]

Name

Although Doyle is often referred to as "Sir Arthur Conan Doyle" or simply "Conan Doyle" (implying that Conan is part of a compound surname, as opposed to a given middle name), his baptism entry in the register of St Mary's Cathedral, Edinburgh, gives "Arthur Ignatius Conan" as his given names, and "Doyle" as his surname. It also names Michael Conan as his godfather.[10] The cataloguers of the British Library and the Library of Congress treat "Doyle" alone as his surname.[11]

Steven Doyle, editor of the Baker Street Journal, has written, "Conan was Arthur's middle name. Shortly after he graduated from high school he began using Conan as a sort of surname. But technically his last name is simply

'Doyle'."[12] When knighted he was gazetted as Doyle, not under the compound Conan Doyle.[13] Nevertheless, the actual use of a compound surname is demonstrated by the fact that Doyle's second wife was known as "Jean Conan Doyle" rather than "Jean Doyle".[14]

Medical career

From 1876 to 1881 he studied medicine at the University of Edinburgh Medical School, including periods working in Aston, Sheffield and Ruyton-XI-Towns, Shropshire.[15] While studying, Doyle began writing short stories. His earliest extant fiction, "The Haunted Grange of Goresthorpe", was unsuccessfully submitted to Blackwood's Magazine.[5] His first published piece, "The Mystery of Sasassa Valley", a story set in South Africa, was printed in Chambers's Edinburgh Journal on 6 September 1879.[5][16] On 20 September 1879, he published his first academic article, "Gelsemium as a Poison" in the British Medical Journal,[5][17][18] a study which the Daily Telegraph regarded as potentially useful in a 21st century alleged murder investigation.[19]

Doyle was employed as a doctor on the Greenland whaler Hope of Peterhead in 1880[20] and, after his graduation from university in 1881 as M.B., C.M., as a ship's surgeon on the SS Mayumba during a voyage to the West African coast.[5] He completed his M.D. degree (an advanced degree in England beyond the usual medical degrees) on the subject of tabes dorsalis in 1885.[21]

In 1882 he joined former classmate George Turnavine Budd as his partner at a medical practice in Plymouth, but their relationship proved difficult, and Doyle soon left to set up an independent practice.[5][22] Arriving in Portsmouth in June 1882 with less than £10 (£900 today[23]) to his name, he set up a medical practice at 1 Bush Villas in Elm Grove, Southsea.[24] The practice was initially not very successful. While waiting for patients, Doyle again began writing fiction.

In 1890 Doyle studied ophthalmology in Vienna, and moved to London, first living in Montague Place and then in South Norwood. He set up a practice as an ophthalmologist at No. 2 Upper Wimpole St, London W1 (then known as 2 Devonshire Place).[25] (A Westminster Council plaque in place over the front door can be seen today.)

Literary career

Sherlock Holmes

Doyle struggled to find a publisher for his work. His first work featuring Sherlock Holmes and Dr. Watson, A Study in Scarlet, was taken by Ward Lock & Co on 20 November 1886, giving Doyle £25 for all rights to the story. The piece appeared later that year in the Beeton's Christmas Annual and received good reviews in The Scotsman and the Glasgow Herald.[5] Holmes was partially modelled on his former university teacher Joseph Bell. Doyle wrote to him, "It is most certainly to you that I owe Sherlock Holmes ... round the centre of deduction and inference and observation which I have heard you inculcate I have tried to build up a man."[26] Dr. (John) Watson owes his surname, but not any other obvious characteristic, to a Portsmouth medical colleague of Doyle's, Dr James Watson.[27]

Robert Louis Stevenson was able, even in faraway Samoa, to recognise the strong similarity between Joseph Bell and Sherlock Holmes: "My compliments on your very ingenious and very interesting adventures of Sherlock Holmes. ... can this be my old friend Joe Bell?"[28] Other authors sometimes suggest additional influences—for instance, the famous Edgar Allan Poe character C. Auguste Dupin.[29]

A sequel to A Study in Scarlet was commissioned and The Sign of the Four appeared in Lippincott's Magazine in February 1890, under agreement with the Ward Lock company. Doyle felt grievously exploited by Ward Lock as an author new to the publishing world and he left them.[5] Short stories featuring Sherlock Holmes were published in the Strand Magazine. Doyle wrote the first five Holmes short stories from his office at 2 Upper Wimpole Street (then known as Devonshire Place), which is now marked by a memorial plaque.[30]

Doyle's attitude towards his most famous creation was ambivalent.[27] In November 1891 he wrote to his mother: "I think of slaying Holmes,... and winding him up for good and all. He takes my mind from better things." His mother responded, "You won't! You can't! You mustn't!".[31] In an attempt to deflect publishers' demands for more Holmes stories, he raised his price to a level intended to discourage them, but found they were willing to pay even the large sums he asked.[27] As a result, he became one of the best-paid authors of his time.

In December 1893, to dedicate more of his time to his historical novels, Doyle had Holmes and Professor Moriarty plunge to their deaths together down the Reichenbach Falls in the story "The Final Problem". Public outcry, however, led him to feature Holmes in 1901 in the novel The Hound of the Baskervilles.

In 1903, Doyle published his first Holmes short story in ten years, The Adventure of the Empty House, in which it was explained that only Moriarty had fallen; but since Holmes had other dangerous enemies—especially Colonel Sebastian Moran—he had arranged to also be perceived as dead. Holmes was ultimately featured in a total of 56 short stories—the last published in 1927—and four novels by Doyle, and has since appeared in many novels and stories by other authors.

Jane Stanford compares some of Moriarty's characteristics to those of the Fenian John O'Connor Power. 'The Final Problem' was published the year the Second Home Rule Bill passed through the House of Commons. 'The Valley of Fear' was serialised in 1914, the year Home Rule, the Government of Ireland Act (18 September) was placed on the Statute Book.[32]

Other works

Doyle's first novels were The Mystery of Cloomber, not published until 1888, and the unfinished Narrative of John Smith, published only in 2011.[33] He amassed a portfolio of short stories including "The Captain of the Pole-Star" and "J. Habakuk Jephson's Statement", both inspired by Doyle's time at sea, the latter of which popularised the mystery of the Mary Celeste and added fictional details such as the perfect condition of the ship (which had actually taken on water by the time it was discovered) and its boats remaining on board (the one boat was in fact missing) that have come to dominate popular accounts of the incident.[1][5]

Between 1888 and 1906, Doyle wrote seven historical novels, which he and many critics regarded as his best work.[27] He also authored nine other novels, and later in his career (1912-1929) five stories, two of novella length, featuring the irascible scientist Professor Challenger. The Challenger stories include what is probably his best-known work after the Holmes oeuvre, The Lost World. He was a prolific author of short stories, including two collections set in Napoleonic times featuring the French character Brigadier Gerard.

Doyle's stage works include Waterloo, the reminiscences of an English veteran of the Napoleonic Wars, the character of Gregory Brewster being written for Henry Irving; The House of Temperley, the plot of which reflects his abiding interest of boxing; The Speckled Band, after the short story of that name; and the 1893 collaboration with J.M. Barrie on the libretto of Jane Annie.[34]

Sporting career

While living in Southsea, Doyle played football as a goalkeeper for Portsmouth Association Football Club, an amateur side, under the pseudonym A. C. Smith.[35] (This club, disbanded in 1896, has no connection with the present-day Portsmouth F.C., which was founded in 1898.) Doyle was a keen cricketer, and between 1899 and 1907 he played 10 first-class matches for the Marylebone Cricket Club (MCC). He also played for the amateur cricket team the Allahakbarries alongside authors J. M. Barrie and A.

A. Milne.[36]

His highest score, in 1902 against London County, was 43. He was an occasional bowler who took just one first-class wicket (although one of the highest pedigree—it was W. G. Grace).[37] Also a keen golfer, Doyle was elected captain of the Crowborough Beacon Golf Club in Sussex for 1910. (He had moved to Little Windlesham house in Crowborough with his second wife, Jean Leckie, living there with his family from 1907 until his death in July 1930.[38])

Personal life

In 1885 Doyle married Mary Louise (sometimes called "Louisa") Hawkins, the youngest daughter of J. Hawkins, of Minsterworth, Gloucestershire, and sister of one of Doyle's patients. She suffered from tuberculosis and died on 4 July 1906.[39] The following year he married Jean Elizabeth Leckie, whom he had first met and fallen in love with in 1897. He had maintained a platonic relationship with Jean while his first wife was still alive, out of loyalty to her.[40] Jean died in London on 27 June 1940.[41]

Doyle fathered five children. He had two with his first wife: Mary Louise (28 January 1889 – 12 June 1976) and Arthur Alleyne Kingsley, known as Kingsley (15 November 1892 – 28 October 1918). He also had three with his second wife: Denis Percy Stewart (17 March 1909 – 9 March 1955), second husband of Georgian Princess Nina Mdivani; Adrian Malcolm (19 November 1910 – 3 June 1970); and Jean Lena Annette (21 December 1912 – 18 November 1997).[42]

Political campaigning

Doyle's house in South Norwood, London
Following the Boer War in South Africa at the turn of the 20th century and the condemnation from some quarters over the United Kingdom's role, Doyle wrote a short work titled The War in South Africa: Its Cause and Conduct,

which justified the UK's role in the Boer War and was widely translated. Doyle had served as a volunteer doctor in the Langman Field Hospital at Bloemfontein between March and June 1900.[43] Doyle believed that this publication was responsible for his being knighted as a Knight Bachelor by King Edward VII in 1902[13] and for his appointment as a Deputy-Lieutenant of Surrey.[44] Also in 1900 he wrote a book, The Great Boer War.

He twice stood for Parliament as a Liberal Unionist—in 1900 in Edinburgh Central and in 1906 in the Hawick Burghs—but although he received a respectable vote, he was not elected.[45] In May 1903 he was appointed a Knight of Grace of the Order of the Hospital of Saint John of Jerusalem.[46]

Doyle was a supporter of the campaign for the reform of the Congo Free State, led by the journalist E. D. Morel and diplomat Roger Casement. During 1909 he wrote The Crime of the Congo, a long pamphlet in which he denounced the horrors of that colony. He became acquainted with Morel and Casement, and it is possible that, together with Bertram Fletcher Robinson, they inspired several characters in the 1912 novel The Lost World.[47] Doyle broke with both Morel and Casement when Morel became one of the leaders of the pacifist movement during the First World War. When Casement was found guilty of treason against the Crown during the Easter Rising, Doyle tried unsuccessfully to save him from facing the death penalty, arguing that Casement had been driven mad and could not be held responsible for his actions.[48]

Justice advocate

Doyle statue in Crowborough, East Sussex
Doyle was also a fervent advocate of justice and personally investigated two closed cases, which led to two men being exonerated of the crimes of which they were accused. The first case, in 1906, involved a shy half-British, half-Indian lawyer named George Edalji who had allegedly penned threatening letters and mutilated animals in Great Wyrley. Police were set on Edalji's conviction, even though the mutilations continued after their suspect was

jailed.[49] Apart from helping George Edalji, Doyle's work helped establish a way to correct other miscarriages of justice, as it was partially as a result of this case that the Court of Criminal Appeal was established in 1907.[50]

The story of Doyle and Edalji was dramatised in an episode of the 1972 BBC television series, The Edwardians. In Nicholas Meyer's pastiche The West End Horror (1976), Holmes manages to help clear the name of a shy Parsi Indian character wronged by the English justice system. Edalji was of Parsi heritage on his father's side. The story was fictionalised in Julian Barnes's 2005 novel Arthur and George, which was adapted into a three-part drama by ITV in 2015.

The second case, that of Oscar Slater, a Yekke and gambling-den operator convicted of bludgeoning an 82-year-old woman in Glasgow in 1908, excited Doyle's curiosity because of inconsistencies in the prosecution case and a general sense that Slater was not guilty. He ended up paying most of the costs for Slater's successful appeal in 1928.[51]

Spiritualism, Freemasonry

One of the five photographs of Frances Griffiths with the alleged fairies, taken by Elsie Wright in July 1917
Doyle had a longstanding interest in mystical subjects. In 1887 he joined the Society for Psychical Research and was also initiated as a Freemason (26 January 1887) at the Phoenix Lodge No 257 in Southsea. He resigned from the Lodge in 1889, but returned to it in 1902, only to resign again in 1911.[52]

Following the death of his wife Louisa in 1906, the death of his son Kingsley just before the end of the First World War, and the deaths of his brother Innes, his two brothers-in-law (one of whom was E. W. Hornung, creator of the literary character Raffles) and his two nephews shortly after the war, Doyle sank into depression. He found solace supporting spiritualism and its attempts to find proof of existence beyond the grave. In particular, according to some,[53] he favoured Christian Spiritualism and encouraged the

Spiritualists' National Union to accept an eighth precept – that of following the teachings and example of Jesus of Nazareth. He was a member of the renowned supernatural organisation The Ghost Club.[54]

Doyle with his family in New York City, 1922

On 28 October 1918, Kingsley Doyle died from pneumonia, which he contracted during his convalescence after being seriously wounded during the 1916 Battle of the Somme. Brigadier-General Innes Doyle died, also from pneumonia, in February 1919. Sir Arthur became involved with Spiritualism to the extent that he wrote a novella on the subject, The Land of Mist, featuring the character Professor Challenger. The Coming of the Fairies (1922)[55] appears to show that Conan Doyle was convinced of the veracity of the five Cottingley Fairies photographs (which decades later were exposed as a hoax). He reproduced them in the book, together with theories about the nature and existence of fairies and spirits.

In 1920, Doyle debated the claims of Spiritualism with the notable sceptic Joseph McCabe at Queen's Hall in London. McCabe later published his evidence against the claims of Doyle and Spiritualism in a booklet entitled Is Spiritualism Based on Fraud? which claimed Doyle had been duped into believing Spiritualism by mediumship trickery.[56]

Doyle was friends for a time with Harry Houdini, the American magician who himself became a prominent opponent of the Spiritualist movement in the 1920s following the death of his beloved mother. Although Houdini insisted that Spiritualist mediums employed trickery (and consistently exposed them as frauds), Doyle became convinced that Houdini himself possessed supernatural powers—a view expressed in Doyle's The Edge of the Unknown. Houdini was apparently unable to convince Doyle that his feats were simply illusions, leading to a bitter public falling out between the two.[57] A specific incident is recounted in memoirs by Houdini's friend Bernard M.L. Ernst, in which Houdini performed an impressive trick at his home in the presence of Conan Doyle. Houdini assured Conan Doyle the trick was pure illusion and that he was attempting to prove a point about Doyle not "endorsing phenomena" simply because he had no explanation. According to Ernst, Conan Doyle refused to believe it was a trick.[58]

In 1922, the psychical researcher Harry Price accused the spirit photographer William Hope of fraud. Doyle defended Hope, but further evidence of trickery was obtained from other researchers.[59] Doyle threatened to have Price evicted from the National Laboratory of Psychical Research and claimed if he persisted to write "sewage" about spiritualists, he would meet the same fate as Harry Houdini.[60] Price wrote "Arthur Conan Doyle and his friends abused me for years for exposing Hope."[61] Because of the exposure of Hope and other fraudulent spiritualists, Doyle led a mass resignation of eighty-four members of the Society for Psychical Research, as they believed the Society was opposed to spiritualism.[62]

Doyle and spiritualist William Thomas Stead were duped into believing Julius and Agnes Zancig had genuine psychic powers, both claiming that the Zancigs used telepathy. In 1924 Julius and Agnes Zancig confessed that that their mind reading act was a trick and published the secret code and all the details of the trick method they had used, under the title Our Secrets!! in a London newspaper.[63] In his book The History of Spiritualism (1926), Doyle praised the psychic phenomena and spirit materializations produced by Eusapia Palladino and Mina Crandon, who were both exposed as frauds.[64] In 1927, Doyle spoke in a filmed interview about Sherlock Holmes and spiritualism.[65]

Doyle in 1930, the year of his death, with his son Adrian
Richard Milner, an American historian of science, has presented a case that Doyle may have been the perpetrator of the Piltdown Man hoax of 1912, creating the counterfeit hominid fossil that fooled the scientific world for over 40 years. Milner says that Doyle had a motive—namely, revenge on the scientific establishment for debunking one of his favourite psychics—and that The Lost World contains several encrypted clues regarding his involvement in the hoax.[66][67] Samuel Rosenberg's 1974 book Naked is the Best Disguise purports to explain how, throughout his writings, Doyle left open clues that related to hidden and suppressed aspects of his mentality.[68]

Death

Doyle's grave at Minstead, England

Doyle was found clutching his chest in the hall of Windlesham Manor, his house in Crowborough, East Sussex, on 7 July 1930. He died of a heart attack at the age of 71. His last words were directed toward his wife: "You are wonderful."[69] At the time of his death, there was some controversy concerning his burial place, as he was avowedly not a Christian, considering himself a Spiritualist. He was first buried on 11 July 1930 in Windlesham rose garden.

He was later reinterred together with his wife in Minstead churchyard in the New Forest, Hampshire.[5] Carved wooden tablets to his memory and to the memory of his wife are held privately and are inaccessible to the public. That inscription reads, "Blade straight/Steel true/Arthur Conan Doyle/Born May 22nd 1859/Passed on 7th July 1930."

The epitaph on his gravestone in the churchyard reads, in part: "Steel true/Blade straight/Arthur Conan Doyle/Knight/Patriot, Physician, and man of letters".[70]

Undershaw, the home near Hindhead, Haslemere, which Doyle had built and lived in between October 1897 and September 1907,[71] was a hotel and restaurant from 1924 until 2004. It was then bought by a developer and stood empty while conservationists and Doyle fans fought to preserve it.[39] In 2012 the High Court ruled the redevelopment permission be quashed because proper procedure had not been followed.[72]

A statue honours Doyle at Crowborough Cross in Crowborough, where he lived for 23 years.[73] There is a statue of Sherlock Holmes in Picardy Place, Edinburgh, close to the house where Doyle was born.[74]

Printed in Great Britain
by Amazon

45714594R00046